I0668314

Description

In this fantasy story the NighT Guardian's family and their spiritual journey is upset by arrival of a daughter conceived during his military service. She is now both a female priest, and warrior of very special ability. Hardened by sometimes brutal experiences from birth, she is driven by a spiritual journey of her own. She is guided and protected by Guardian Angels who speak to her through her intuition. She brings to the family political and military intrigue, doubts, and questions which tests their faith and breaks the peace of their lives. This is book one in the NighT Guardian Series, click on the link to purchase and immerse yourself in the adventure.

The NighT Guardian gazed to the west for the first orange glimmers of Day Rise but did not see any. The last of three moons had long since left the sky to the east, he flipped the lip of the pouch that hung off his belt and felt for a piece of root.

Cavahn, his spouse, cut the root into small pieces so he could snack slowly on them through the night. Unlike the spouses of other NighT Guardian's his did not cut the root into pieces of equal size, some were large, some were small, the last one had been small, too small. It had dissolved on his tongue too quickly and had been slightly bitter; she must have left some ground soil on it. He had washed the taste away with clear fresh river liquid from his flask. But, he had observed on a few occasions that he had more root than the others even though it was not cut into equal pieces.

And there in he saw the wisdom and purpose of it. If the pieces were uneven it was not possible for others to easily see that he had been provided with more root than anyone else and that as a result he was probably better wealthed than other NighT Guardians. Wealth partly inherited and partly gained as a commander in the bloody service of The Vanguard of the Imperial Black Guard.

The Vanguard was always first into battle and last to leave the field, sometimes thrown behind enemy lines as a distraction and with no hope of relief they would always fight relentlessly and remorselessly for the Emperor.

He looked down from his Watchtower at the eight red shaded lanterns winding their way through the prison grounds. The executioners were hurrying home from the execution grounds. Their work done, like those who they had executed, they must not see the first glimmer of Day Rise on the day of execution. The difference being the executioners would see the next Day Rise, and the one after that, those they had left on the ground would not.

The NighT Guardian picked another small piece of root and started to chew it. His attention slowly switching between the red lanterns as they swung back and forth on the executioner's poles and the first faint glimmer of Day Rise off to the west. The executioners walked in a deep depression where Day Rise would not reach for several minutes after it had illuminated the NighT Guardian's Watchtower.

Somewhere in the woods north of the prison a tree fell followed by a gnawing cry. A Vanmor had felled a tree, it was preparing for the bright days of Great Warmth. Without proper shelter, the Great Warmth of twin suns during the summer period would make being outside only barely tolerable. Thinking of the coming season, the NighT Guardian pulled his cloak closer to his neck as protection against the heat of summer months too come.

He looked down the steps of his Watchtower, a round young face looked up to the NighT Guardian's platform, and he saw a young hand on the railing and a foot on the first rung. The NighT Guardian tapped the floor of his position with the end of his staff and both hand and foot retreated, the face disappeared for a moment in a deferential bow and then returned to look up.

The NighT Guardian tapped the floor again and the mouth in the round face opened.

"NighT Guardian! The Layers are ready."

As Senior NighT Guardian he had the option to inspect and choose from the possessions of those to be executed, trinkets and such they had brought with them into the prison or that their family had given to them during their stay. He had selected a pendant and a ring. The pendant would be an easy and valuable sale in the market. The ring he would give to the young one with the round face at the base of his Watchtower. He had spoken to the Layers, priests, who laid out the possessions of those just executed to make sure he received the two pieces and that they did not find their way to the Day Guardians who were starting to relieve the night watch.

The NighT Guardian turned to the West; the first glimmers of Day Rise were spreading between the Great Mountains on either side of the wide flat even valley through which the River Ohm flowed. The river now had a faint golden tinge to it in the far, very far, distance. He looked down at the red lanterns, as he did, the last one passed through a faintly lighted door. The Executioners were safe.

Along a winding path he could see three-Day Guardians walking to his position. They walked heavily; they carried extra cloaks, gloves and wore heavier boots. They carried visors and bundles of food and extra river liquid that would protect and carry them through the heat of the day to come. With twin suns in the sky, the heat at the mid point of a summers day could burn an inadequately protected Day Guardian, or anyone else not properly shielded.

The last of the Day Guardians arrived at the first rung of the ladder to his Watch Tower. The change between NighT and Day Guardian was about to take place. The young round face stepped back to give witness.

With the Day Guardian looking upwards and his staff held in front of him, the NighT Guardian turned sideways to the Day Rise and the deepening golden colour of the River Ohm. The NighT Guardian, fiercely tapped the floor of his watchtower with his staff and held out his left arm pointing to the Day Rise as if it were an enemy and he was giving warning about it and direction of the threat. Then he laid the staff along his out stretched arm, lengthening and emphasizing the direction in which he was giving warning.

The Day Guardian threw back his hood to better see in which direction the enemy was coming and wrapped the bottom rung of the ladder three times that he understood. The NighT Guardian looked down at a familiar face, a face scared from being out in the Great Warmth of summer in the southern lands, this Day Guardian knew what it was to be out at mid day and to be unprotected. The NighT and Day Guardian looked at each other for a long moment or recognition and then the Day Guardian wrapped the bottom rung of the watchtower ladder another three times more to signify he accepted responsibility for the threat. He replaced his hood and stood aside as the NighT Guardian walked down the ladder.

To ensure The Guardianship was handed over securely the NighT Guardian watched the Day Guardian climb to the watchtower platform and place his food and river liquid in a niche in the wall to protect it from the heat of middle Day Rise.

The change of Guardian was good; now the NighT Guardian could leave. He turned to the young round face that would some day be a NighT Guardian. "Let's go see the Layers." At that moment another tree fell in the woods, the falling tree was accompanied with a wild gnawing sound. Their attention momentarily directed northwards, "It looks like it will be a very warm summer, my Young Guardian." They moved off along the path the Day Guardian had taken.

In the space between the outer high wall where the NighT Guardian held his post and the Battle Castle of the Empower where the prison existed, numerous buildings had sprung up, almost, but not quite a small village similar to one you might find along the River Ohm. In the buildings the functions and business of the castle and its defenses at both the inner and outer walls were carried out with no need to cross into the castle proper and so reducing the number of people who had knowledge of the inner defenses and workings of the castle.

The NighT Guardian had never been inside the castle but he knew his title of NighT Guardian at the Prison was a piece of disinformation the Emperor spread about. Yes, the prison existed inside the castle and that is how the castle was known but in reality the castle's main function was the place where the Emperor lived and held court. As the Emperors residence it was an inviting target for those who were restless, but as a prison, not so much.

They left the main path and now followed another that abruptly turned downhill to a long low building with heavy shutters that were propped open to allow in the cool night breeze. The shutters could be closed easily at the height of Day Rise when the temperature was at it greatest, trapping the cool air inside. And, like his own house, a major part of the building was inside the small hill they were now navigating around, there was also a long, deep overhang shielding the front the building and the open shutters from full Day Rise and the fierce temperatures of the coming summer season. Inside the mostly buried building, its rooms would be cool and comfortable.

At a heavy wooden door they stopped. The NighT Guardian looked at the Young Guardian. He was already in prayer to his guardian spirits. Feet closely pressed together, head bowed a slight murmur coming from his throat and his hands balled in to fists pressed together in front of him. It was right, they should prey at the door before entering to select possessions from those who had been executed, and the NighT Guardian momentarily assumed the same penitent position, also praying to the spirits that guarded and guided him in total silence. No sound came from his throat. As a member of the Vanguard he had seen men die when vocalizing their prayers before battle.

The keen ears of a trained Vanmor could seek out sounds such as a human voice at great distance allowing their handler to launch a missile at the spot the animal indicated and kill whoever was making the sound. He must tell the Young Guardian not to make such sounds when praying.

The NighT Guardian tapped the door with his staff at the top right corner, next to the heavy metal hinge and then left at the bottom, twice and then twice again.

The door slowly opened revealing a middle aged woman dressed in the dark and light blue robes of a priest. She looked at the two Guardians and bowed her head, hands balled into fists tightly pressed together. As her lips moved invoking a prayer to all the spirits present between them, no sound came from her throat. The NighT Guardian knew why there was no sound when she prayed. They met on the last campaign the NighT Guardian had fraught before retiring from the Vanguard, she had served as one of the priests to the Vanguard, administering last worship to the fallen and helping guide their spirits to the next life, she had helped preserve the guardian spirits of the wounded and assisted the healers nurse their physical bodies back to health.

She had seen with her own eyes men fall dead for praying too loudly before the start of battle. Dead they were before even engaging the enemy; such was the power of the Vanmor and their skilled handlers.

When she looked up her hands slipped by her sides and where the long sleeves of her robes covered them. After a suitable period, the NighT Guardian held out his hands for blessing, palms facing upwards to the heavens.

The priest stepped forward reached out, her palms facing down to rest on the NighT Guardians hands. Their eyes locked and a short silent prayer of blessing each other's spirits was said. He felt the warmth of the priest's right hand on his but on the left he felt a small square of cloth. The cloth was not flat; it was a pouch containing things that were hard and angular. The pendant and the ring he had selected earlier. As their hands slid over each other at the end of the prayer, the NighT Guardian secured the pouch of cloth without the Young Guardian standing just a few steps away seeing. In a moment the pouch was inside the long sleeves of his cloak in a natural and easy movement.

The priest stood aside holding out a welcoming arm beckoning them to enter. In clear voice she welcomed them with the traditional greeting by a priest to those entering a place of worship, "Enter First NighT Guardian, all that come after shall not see and experience what you shall see and know first."

Inside, lighting globes hovered above eight tables, one for each person executed that morning, the tables were covered with dark and light blue cloth that matched the colours of the priest's robes. Behind each table a young priest stood, clothed in the same coloured robes. The NighT Guardian's boots sounded heavy and out of place in the exquisite silence of the room. The footfalls of the Young Guardian were soft in comparison.

The NighT Guardian stopped and looked back at the Young Guardian who was at a table examining something attractive but worthless. He looked down at the young man's feet, they were covered with thick rags and dry animal-feed straw from the stables – he needed boots, which the ring would not entirely pay for when sold in the market.

The NighT Guardian moved on slowly allowing the Young Guardian to catch up and see what he was doing. On the last table the NighT Guardian picked up a metal drinking vessel decorated with engraved animals from the East and North. He bowed to the young priest behind the table who returned his bow. The drinking vessel entered the Nigh Guardians robes and he moved on towards the door at the end of the building. The Young Guardian returned to the table where the attractive, worthless trinket continued to fascinate him.

At the exit the priest looked at the NighT Guardian with an expression that asked the question "why the ring, pendant and the drinking vessel?" Reading the unvoiced question the NighT Guardian pointed to the Young Guardian's feet. "He needs boots that the ring alone will not buy." The priest looked in the direction of the Young Guardian and at his feet, "What is left from a life that has ended becomes a blessing to those who live" she said, and marked the ending word with a hand sign that told the NighT Guardian he and his intended deed were good in the eyes of the priest.

The NighT Guardian tapped the floor with his staff to attract the Young Guardian's attention. Clearly the young man wanted to take the worthless trinket with him but the demeanor of the NighT Guardian indicated they were leaving and nothing else would be tolerated. He left the trinket on the table and hurried to the exit where the priest blessed him and closed the door behind him, he joined the NighT Guardian outside.

The NighT Guardian looked up at the towers of the Battle Castle and the inner defensive wall, they were just tinged with the orange glow of first Morning Rise. The NighT Guardian turned abruptly to the path that led to the outer gate through which they would pass.

The path down to the village was steep and winding, purposefully so, the defenders above could rain death and destruction on anyone they did not want to approach the prison.

The first quarter rim of first sun had broken the horizon by the time they stood in front of the boot maker. The NighT Guardian gestured with his staff at the feet of the Young Guardian. The boot maker studied the feet for a moment and named a price. The NighT Guardian wrapped the front of the boot maker's table sharply with his staff making the boot maker shake visibly, and the price fell steeply to one the NighT Guardian agreed as reasonable. The NighT Guardian took out the drinking vessel and handed it to the boot maker who studied it, the boot maker looked up and indicated it was not enough.

The NighT Guardian dropped the ring into the vessel, the boot maker studied the ring carefully and finally he gestured to a wall of sample boots; some of which had harder, tougher soles, some had reinforced uppers, and some went up to the knee and added protection to the front of the leg and the knee.

The Young Guardian indicated he wanted tougher soles and uppers. The boot maker nodded to the NighT Guardian and the deal was done. In all this barter, the NighT Guardian had said not a word, his presence, his stature, and countenance had spoken for him; only the boot maker had spoken. Even the Young Guardian had said nothing; only pointing to the sample boots that had features he wanted made in his.

The NighT Guardian left the Young Guardian with the boot maker taking measurements. It would not take long to make the boots, maybe the rest of the day. The young man could spend his time getting a good meal and sleeping in one of the special lodges the Guardians used when in the village.

The NighT Guardian turned left from the boot maker's shop and walked down the cobbled street towards the River Ohm, eventually the street turned into a series of paths, the NighT Guardian took one less travelled and that path turned into several more, one led to a break in the foliage and trees that lined all the paths down here close to the river, once through the trees he was on a path that would take him to his house and his spouse.

The River Ohm was fed by huge amounts of winter snow and ice that fell for months in the bitterly cold Great Mountains to the far north and even further east, he had seen the lands and mountains covered with this white flakey frozen liquid once on a tour of duty with the Vanguard. As the seasons changed and the air warmed and the days grew longer, the snow melted and turned into river liquid that flowed in many violent, deep angry rivers and passed through gorges and passes until it fell in five great tower-falls that brought all the river liquid together in to what he knew as the River Ohm. Then it flowed through the valley and by the time it reached the NighT Guardian's house the river was very, very, wide and flowing slowly, the air was laden with moisture and cool here.

As he walked across the grass to his home the remnants of ground moisture from the previous night covered his boots. There were wild flowers closer to his house, organized flower patterns and trees trimmed with flowering buds that brightened the view from the second level of his home.

Like most his house only displayed its front and had a very large overhang that shaded the verandah of the two levels beneath it, facing the cool river a person could sit out and enjoy the river and the scenery from either level while being protected from the burning heat of twin suns. And like most buildings what you saw as you approached was only part of it; eleven rooms and a training room had been built into the hill behind the house for shelter against the heat that bore down from the skies. As he walked up the narrow path to his home he could see Cavahn standing on the second level waving to him. She was dressed in the long dark maroon dress with purple and gold braid rope that defined her in part as coming from the western lands, the far, very far west, the place where all land met the Great Salt Sea, it also marked her as a member of a holy order.

They had met when he was fighting in the Vanguard to subdue the great western families that had determined to oppose the Emperor. The last battle had been fought and he had taken to swimming in the Great Salt Sea. He would swim and sometimes wedge himself against a rock and let the small fish nibble away at the scars and scabs on his body. The salt water was wonderful for his open wounds and cuts, and the small fish ate the dried blood and dead skin hungrily.

From such a rock he had watched the first sailboat he had ever seen depart from the near by harbour. He had seen sailboats on the River Ohm, and on lakes when he campaigned in the North, but none were as big and mighty as these that sailed to far off lands across the sea.

He had seen her from where he was swimming. In the west you did not have to worry about the great heat because the sea so moderated the temperature. She was standing like a tall slim statue on the shore next to a pile of clothes that was his uniform. She was wearing a long Maroon dress with maroon cape edged with blue and gold braided rope and a round broad rimmed hat trimmed with gold rope.

He emerged from the sea naked and stood before her looking at her red liquid eyes and red tinged hair that defined her as coming from a religious cast that supported none of the families that had fought against the Emperor. She stooped to give him one by one the pieces of his uniform. She only stopped to look at the Honour Ribbons that decorated the left breast of his jacket.

He hoped to impress her and asked if he could describe them to her but instead, she described them to him, down to the minutest detail of each circumstance that led to the award as if she had read the proclamation that came with the honour. He had asked if she had read the announcements and she said no. He asked if she were telepathic, and asked if she were reading his mind, she said no. He asked if she had spoken to members of the Vanguard about him and she said no.

She told him she knew all of him that a spouse would need to know.

He had protested that he was not looking for a spouse, he was still in the Vanguard and dedicated to fight where the Emperor needed him and to die if required.

She simply looked at him with her red liquid eyes and an expression that told him that it did not matter. He had the feeling that his life would be changing, evolving, and soon.

She had held out a slim hand with long, slender fingers and he held them gently. Her fingers tightened and for the first time since he was cut in the last battle he flinched, he grimaced at her grip on his hand. He felt something like the energy that powers lighting globes pass from her grip to his hand, his forearm tensed and then his biceps twitched angrily, then, his shoulder shuddered as it did when plunging a blade into an enemy and hitting bone.

Within the month the Vanguard left the far western lands. They had married and she was carrying the first of their five children.

Of those five children, two girls; K'ola and Invar had joined the Vanguard, K'ola, the oldest assuming his commanders role, while Invar was leader of a group dedicated to swift decisive strikes at the enemy from behind their lines. The third daughter, Vella, was a healer in the Black Legion. The two boys, Callar and Lovan were in Imperial service and he assumed they were spies but he knew not where they were, he suspected one, Callar, was in the north, the other in the east, past the mountains that helped give birth to the River Ohm.

As he neared the house, he could see footsteps had created a faint trail in the ground moisture from the previous night. He followed the trail with his eyes down to the thick tall reeds that grew down by the river; it was from those reeds that Cavahn harvested the root she prepared for his snacks. But the trail he thought could have another purpose, which made him smile.

When he reached the front door it was open and Cavahn nowhere to be seen. This was normal. Western women and especially members of her worshipful cast did not wait by the door to welcome their mate home and watch him perform basic tasks like taking off boots, removing and hanging up their cloak or putting their staff in the special niche by the door.

She did not make an appearance when he walked barefoot to the kitchen to leave the pouch in which she placed the roots for him to snack on. Instead she was in the living room sanctifying two glasses of river liquid so clear that at first glance you would have thought the glasses were empty. She held out one glass to him which he took in the opposite hand to which she gave it.

They linked arms and locked their gaze in each other eyes and slowly, over several minutes, drank the cool clear cool consecrated liquid. They placed the glasses back on the table and embraced, kissing passionately and relentlessly. When they stopped kissing they held on to each other desperately so each could catch their breath.

From the night of their wedding, to now, this had been their ritual. The passion was never lost; at the beginning it was raw, draining, now it was like the heat from the twin suns at the height of summer, fierce, and constant, impossible to escape and only just in balance with their ability to live with it.

As their breath steadied, they moved apart, slowly. Hands that had held each other's head as they kissed moved down to shoulders and then to arms, to hands and finally, reluctantly finger tips slipped over each other and parted.

From a pocket the NighT Guardian palmed the small cloth pouch containing the pendant. Cavahn took the pouch and tipped out the pendant onto her left hand, her knife hand. She held it up by the full length of the gold chain and looked at the intricately carved and engraved gold teardrop, inside the outer shell, a second gold teardrop could be seen through delicate cut outs.

She knew the NighT Guardian did not know from whom the pendant came. Although he had selected it while the owner still lived, he was forbidden from knowing them.

Cavahn studied the engraving under the light of a lighting globe turned to high. Turning it over and over in her hand, she held it up again and then slowly carefully rolled the teardrop until a broad smile appeared on her beautiful face.

She beckoned the NighT Guardian and carefully placed the teardrop in his scarred hands. "Look!' she exclaimed, "They look like ornaments, one within the other, each beautifully engraved but when you align the inner teardrop correctly with cut outs in the outer shell, the designs become one! It is from the East and South East. The inner teardrop is a minor house in the southeast, House Covanta. The outer teardrop is House Fergal from farther east. House Fergal is a larger, stronger house but…" And she held up the pendant again to let it swing in the air.

The inner teardrop made a pleasant chiming sound as it tapped against the outer shell. Cavahn smiled. "House Fergal consumed Covanta, its lands, people, riches and the noble family and House Covanta carry the colours and banners of Fergal but Covanta still exists, it works inside of Fergal."

"Like those other things I brought home?" he asked.

"When the designs are aligned they make one, which is how we have been taught to see the politics of one house consuming another." She set the pendant down and walked to a long heavy cabinet decorated with ornate carvings and displaying family mementoes and decorations of their dynasty. She reached to the back and touched a piece of decoration and then another and another.

A concealed drawer popped open. He knew it well; they had used it many times while they had been returning from the western lands after they married. Even within the Vanguard not everyone could be trusted and all members of the Vanguard had a hiding place of some kind.

Cavahn took the drawer to the table and waved over another lighting globe and turned it to full. The draw contained several things but at one end, a silk cloth was wrapped around something. She laid the cloth open on the table. Inside were two other beautifully decorated pieces. One a sleek black writing instrument exquisitely carved with intricate design. Where a writer would hold the instrument it was decorated with great beauty and precision and revealed through delicate metal work a slender rod inside, also decorated with great beauty. The instrument was not made entirely of gold; instead it was made of volcanic rock with flecks of gold embedded.

Cavahn rolled the writing instrument back and forth watching the rod inside align and realign with the design on its casing. Then she stopped. The inner rod and outer casing had aligned. They stared at it. "House Brancon working inside House Pelcor" she said.

She then took out what looked like a shape puzzle on a golden chain. She let the long chain dangle free of her hands. She stopped and considered the puzzle pieces. She considered the gold chain on which the pieces moved. She started to complete the design. The small gold shapes connected and reconnected at the end of her slender fingers. Then she flipped the puzzle pieces over so she was looking at the back and started the puzzle again. Then stopped, frustrated.

The NighT Guardian knew better than to speak when Cavahn was in this mind frame. Her liquid red eyes closed, Cavahn was breathing evenly but deeply. Her fingers running slowly back and forth over the back and front of the puzzle pieces then her eyes opened and she smiled. "Look! Small indentations and rough spots, but not on all of the pieces." She took his fingers and rubbed them over the pieces, "Yes, I can feel them now." "I thought it was just wear," he said.

She lay the puzzle down on the silk cloth and moved the pieces according to the indentations and rough spots. The pieces that were not needed she moved to the far end of the gold loop. The rough and indented pieces fell into two interlocking circles and so did the designs engraved on each piece. She expelled a deep breath. "House Koru inside House Mahan." She looked at him out of the corner of her eye she wanted to make sure he understood. She pointed to the two circles… "Look how the circles interlock, Koru on the bottom, Mahan on the top, both as it should be but where they overlap, House Koru engravings are in the top circle where those of House Mahan should be."

The NighT Guardian moved closer, his shoulder touching Cavahn's as he looked down on the completed puzzle. Now that they had the three pieces next to each other he pointed to each in turn and then made a large circle in the air, encompassing them all. "These are from people who have been executed over the past several months of winter and spring."

Cavahn gripped the edge of the table, leaning slightly forward deep in thought. "They are all minor houses that have been defeated or swallowed by a more powerful house, a house that has assumed their lands, wealth and armies. She stood up and ran her fingers through her long red tinged hair and stared at him. "Is it as simple as wealth and armies?" He said nothing. She continued, "If the houses are reforming themselves and their internal balance of power is changing, it could be very dangerous for the Emperor."

He drew out a chair and sat down. "If the Emperor were to attack what he thought was a major house and the forces were elsewhere, commanded by what tradition says was a lesser, defeated house, that should no longer existed, he could be defeated."

Then, she gently ran her fingers over the three objects, studying them again. She pointed to the writing instrument. "All of these are highly intricate, the writing instrument shows the most wear, it has been well used," she said. "This has been happening for quite a while, perhaps before we came back from the west and our first was birthed." She continued, "None of these are plain objects, they are made from valuable metals beautifully grafted to hide their message in plain sight."

The NighT Guardian was silent for a moment. "I have no way of knowing who the owner was, or how they came to be in the prison." He tapped his fingers on the table as he continued to think. "All the lands and houses are remote. When I campaigned in the east I only heard of Mahan and Koru, I did not meet anyone from them and we did not fight them." His voice trailed off. "But why display the message at all?" he asked.

"The answer to that is difficult," Cavahn replied.

Although it was obviously connected with power and influence, the Senate, the Emperor, armies and raw wealth the NighT Guardian was not one to care too much about these things. Although he had possessed considerable stature in the Vanguard it was as a leader and organizer of men and ultimately a warrior on the front line. Now, serving as Senior NighT Guardian at the prison his time was less stressful and a good deal less dangerous. "We don't know why it was decided the owners of these things would be executed. Or, more correctly, what their execution will convey to their Houses." The NighT Guardian said on a flat and slightly bored tone.

Then Cavahn changed the subject. "How well do you know the priest that laid out the pendant or any of these items? Was it the same one each time?" she asked.

He tapped the pendant, "She was in the Vanguard, a priest, healer and Burial Warden. She did not give me the other two pieces. There was a different Layer with each of them. Only tonight did I ask for specific pieces. The others were laid out with the executed persons possessions, I took them as I passed through the room." He looked at Cavahn who was already carefully wrapping the pieces in the silk cloth and putting them in the drawer. She placed the hidden drawer into its hiding place.

"No more trinkets until we know more!" she said.

"Agreed" said the NighT Guardian.

The NighT Guardian ran his hands over the inside of the reed dome Cavahn had made deep in the very tall reeds down by the river. She had taught him how to make the dome by bending over the reeds and lacing them together so that they staid in place and were thick enough to protect against the twin suns. Over the years there had been a great many such domes constructed.

It was their habit since shortly after the birth of their second child, Invar, to hide in a dome down by the river. They would run, or walk down from the house leave food and wine in the dome and swim naked in the cool gentle water by the reeds. The river water caused a breeze to flow through the dome, keeping them cool even in the height of Summer Heat.

She lay next to him, as naked as he, breathing easily, her eyes closed. In the dome they would drink the wine, eat a meal, and copulate vigorously for hours. Three of their five children had been conceived in such a dome.

She ran her hand over his chest and lightly scratched at it. "Thoughts?"

He took her hand and kissed each of her fingers in turn. "I am thinking we have not seen any of our children for some time." He said. Her mouth was a few short measures from his ear; he heard the warm light chuckle in her throat. "Are you worried about the trinkets?" she asked.

"No, sort of, maybe" was his uncertain answer.

"We could consign them to the river, I am sure it has disposed of much worse and larger than those little things. There is a bigger question, are you worried for our children, or because of our children?" She asked.

He thought for a moment about the implications of the question. "I cannot judge the question, or answer it without thinking of the children, they are adults now, they have been molded by forces and people outside of our knowledge" and he paused. He rolled on his side to face her. As he did her red liquid eyes opened to meet his gaze.

She finished the sentence… "…Even if it were against their own parents?" There was silence for several minutes.

"They would be able to justify any action." He said rather flatly and disappointed that it had taken him so long to come to that conclusion. "Perhaps I should have said that as soon K'ola joined the Vanguard, then took my old post as commander so quickly."

Cavahn sat up and turned away from him. She picked up the bag in which they brought their food and wine, and placed it between her legs. "No one that I have heard has said we did not parent five incredibly intelligent children who would excel at anything they tried." She took out a small preserve jar and placed it between them. Inside he recognized the silk cloth. He did not touch the jar. She opened it and laid out the silk cloth on the reed floor and then placed each of the three trinkets on the cloth. After a few minutes passed in silence she rewrapped the pieces in the cloth and placed everything back in the jar. She held a hand over the open mouth of the jar and meditated for a moment. She looked at him, "I asked my guiding spirits to remove any and all spiritual attachments or strands from these objects. These are now just things that man has made." She looked around at the edge of the dome and picked up several rocks that had been cleared aside to make the floor of the dome comfortable and added them to the jar and then sealed it.

"When we were swimming under the surface, do you remember the small ledge? The one that goes back further than an arms length?" There were some stone rocks there that could be moved to close off the ledge." Their eyes met. He nodded.

They slipped out of the dome and within a few seconds were in the cool water. Facing each other they inhaled deeply at the same moment and then slipped under the surface of the water.

They broke the surface just moments apart, wiping water and strands of hair from their faces she made a small hand sign to the NighT Guardian, it was done. He nodded. Now that the pieces of jewelry were away from the house and in a place where they could easily be forgotten, he felt relieved.

He drew her to him and kissed her. They swam ashore and crawled back into the dome, inside she pushed him and he rolled over face up, she was on him in a moment. The suns had only just reached their highest point in the sky, and so had their raw passion for each other.

They emerged from the reeds well after First Sun had left the sky and second Sun was partly obscured by the high mountains to the East. The fierce heat of Mid Day Summer Heat was gone, and the coolness of the coming night was starting to spread up the river valley.

Ahead in the house they could see Lighting globes alight that had not been turned on when they left. She took his hand, "Speak second, to their first, and think like a commander in battle." The NighT Guardian murmured his approval.

Husband and spouse moved easily through the front door and looked to the dinning room from where the light emanated. Before them stood Vella, their third daughter, tall like her mother with the same slender hands and fingers. She too had the liquid red eyes of her mother but these where flecked with blue from her father. Her hair like her mother's was rich, long and abundant but not so red. It was a softer red with some brown also from her father. A Healer in the Imperial Black Legion she was not wearing her uniform. Instead she wore a long maroon skirt in deference to her mother' caste and a white shirt of light, very finely woven cloth, the cuffs on the sleeves were black as was the collar in deference to her position in the Black Legion.

Mother and daughter's hands flashed in a silent message of greeting and gratitude for seeing each other and the joining of their guiding spirits. The NighT Guardian could read the messages exchanged by the rapidly moving hands but his were not so effective or as fast. As his daughter turned to him the words they exchanged were simpler and less elaborate but nonetheless loving and caring of each other's spirits. The exchanges spoke of manifesting peace and love for their soul and spirit guides of the person reading them. The silent hand gestures were in response to and from a time when such expressions were outlawed and anyone overhearing a greeting was obliged to expose the speaker to agents of the Grand Marshal. As the messages finished, they all smiled and Vella rounded the table she had been preparing for their dinner and hugged and kissed each of them in turn. "When I found the home empty, I knew you two were down in the reeds… Are you thinking of starting another family?" she asked, with a mischievous smile on her face. "Should I prepare for more sisters and brothers?"

Cavahn threw back her head in laughter and looked at her spouse. "I have born five children and still have my figure, another five and I would certainly loose it!" she exclaimed.

Vella, still grinning "Well, just saying! Both of you are less than half way through your lives; you could, easily, if you wanted to, start another generation."

At that, the NighT Guardian excused himself as mother and daughter; arm in arm went to the verandah to sit at the large table and talk.

As the male head of the family, the NighT Guardian sat to the right of the female head of the family who took the chair at the head of the table. Vella sat across from the NighT Guardian as the eldest child present. A mix of lighting globes turned to the lower, warmer, end of their spectrum hovered high in the ceiling, on side tables candles flickered giving the room a comforting, intimate glow.

Around this table had sat parents and five children. They had celebrated birthdays, festivals, life passage rituals and it was here they had meditated and learned to talk to their soul and its guardian spirits. They had considered their life's purpose and how to fulfill it. Between them, warmer plates kept bowls of food at eating temperature. At the end of the table cold plates kept the deserts cold. Cavahn was an excellent cook but Vella had taken the knowledge and skills Cavahn had provided and molded them into something new surpassing her mother's abilities.

As the meal progressed, each person sampled complex mixtures of warm food from different bowls and plates as they talked. They talked little of the past. Vella was now an accredited and senior healer with the Emperor's premier legion, The Imperial Black Legion, recounting stories of her running naked from the river through a bridal party celebrating at their home, or worse, on one occasion, a funeral, were not appropriate and not needed, those past happenings were for childhood remembrances and frankly right now, a little stale.

As they chatted happily back and forth, and like the cold deserts they would soon share, there was a growing feeling that important things had to be discussed and that all that was happening was a prelude to what was to come. The cold deserts were a mix of silky smooth textures and delicious flavours mixed with nuts and seeds that had been roasted and which now provided a hard crunch and surprising pop as they bit into them.

Finally, each of them in turn crossed their utensils across the plate they had used throughout the dinner, pushed it away and sat back in their chairs and meditated on the bounty they had just consumed.

Life was good.

The NighT Guardian broke the silence after each had concluded their thoughts. "By all accounts Vella, you have journeyed from very far to the east, somewhere, they say, beyond where the twin suns set before the start of each night. Why?" Rituals of small talk and subtle probing to get answers was not a feature of the NighT Guardian's family as he grew up and Cavahn had come to appreciate what some would see as bluntness in such direct questions.

Cavahn turned to face her daughter who was silent and patient in her answer. Vella would not be rushed, her response was to roll up her left sleeve to reveal the tattoo of the Black Legion. She drew their attention to the tattoo by running her long slender fingers over it. "The Black Legion has been defeated. It happened several months ago but word of it has been suppressed. On the face of it, the losses have been made good from soldiers of lesser Legions, the Black Legion looks complete, but it is a shell."

The NighT Guardian opened his mouth to speak but Cavahn held up her right hand to stop him. "How are your sisters?" She asked calmly. "Were they with the Vanguard when this happened?"

Vella looked at her mother and then her father in turn. "K'ola was wounded in several engagements over the course of a moon cycle, small skin cuts and bruises, nothing to be concerned about. In the last fight, it was different, she was seriously injured." Vella paused, looking at her parents for some sign they wanted to ask questions, but no words were said, her parents looked at her patiently. "K'ola was brought to my healing station where I treated her and brought her spirit and her fitness back to her. She sends her deepest love to you both. Invar is still with the Vanguard and is well, she was credited with many actions against the Mahan and Koru and commands in the Vanguard to this day. She also sends her very deepest love to you both"

Then Vella rose from her chair and walked around the table to the NighT Guardian and from a pocket took a slim black case that was polished to the highest possible level. It appeared to have no hinges and no way of opening it. His daughter ran her finger along the length of the case from end to end and slowly a seam appeared and the case opened. The top part moved up and to the side and then carefully Vella disengaged it from the bottom. Inside, the bottom half was lined with gold except for one end that was burnished black moonstone flecked with gold. On the black moonstone rested three disks made of the finest Kalen shell mounted on three filigree bars of black gold. His daughter placed the two halves of the case on the able between her parents and slowly walked around to her seat and sat down.

Both parents stared at the award in front of them. The three disks symbolized the twin moons and the smaller third moon, often referred to as the "child moon" that rose every night to give the world a clean, pure light, free of the blazingly bright suns of the day. Each moon and each disk in the award had a distinctive colour, not unlike the pal pink, yellow and blue of the leaves of the Stolle tree at the end of the hot season and before the cool winter months spread across the lands. The black moonstone flecked with gold represented the night sky populated with stars. The gold lining symbolized the wealth and importance of recognition. This was an award that was so rarely given that in some centuries none would be conferred. In other centuries none who received the award would be living.

Vella broke the silence with a subdued voice. "K'ola is the only living person and the third this century to hold the award. She confers it to you both." She paused, and then leaned forward as if what she was saying was in confidence though there was no one who could have overheard what she was to say. "It was presented by the Emperor at my healing station. After, the generals and the Imperial Court left, K'ola, alone, spoke with the Emperor for over an hour."

The NighT Guardian looked at his daughter rather harshly. "This award is proclaimed. Parents and family are presented with an imperial notification to attend the ceremony which is held in front of the full court." He looked at Cavahn, "Neither of us have been notified, there was no proclamation. From what you say, the Imperial Court was not present to give witness."

Vella wrapped her arms around herself as if hugging herself. "There was no notification to you and there was no proclamation but it has been recorded in the Roles of Honour." She looked at both parent in turn, "I checked" she said.

Cavahn looked at the award and then to Vella, "This award is connected to the defeat of the Black Legion, isn't it? This has to do with some special act of bravery K'ola performed that saved the Black Legion from total annihilation and it cannot be proclaimed without the fate of the Legion being known."

Vella sat back in her chair, her arms now limp on it armrests. Her hands at the end of the armrests fidgeted." In the senate for the past several months the major houses from the east have been aligning and realigning in complex shifts of power. Ultimately resulting in the Emperor losing control of the houses that have long provided him with leverage and control in the east." She paused, "In response the Emperor moved the Black Legion and Vanguard to the east." She paused again, longer this time, "House Mahan was... Is... the centre of disruption in the east, when the Emperor moved against Mahan, the forces he attacked were a shell, he chased them deeper and deeper into Mahan lands until he could no longer properly supply the Legion, or the Vanguard and they both became separated from each other and their supplies." Vella heaved a long nervous breath before continuing, "Vastly superior forces from what had been Koru lands attacked the Legion repeatedly, spies murdered many officers and commanders of the Legion and Vanguard. Supplies for both were also destroyed."

Vella looked at the NighT Guardian with a hard stare, "The Black Legion and the Vanguard may be exceptional fighters, strong, fierce, remorseless and tough but they have never starved, they have never been without water or shelter from the heat of the day," she paused. "The shade tents were burned early on in the campaign by the spies, the soldiers were unprotected during Day Rise."

Vella stopped to let this sink in. "Both of my sisters led the Vanguard and the Legion in many actions against the Koru and eventually provided what was left of the Vanguard, and Legion, along with the Emperor with an escape route. It was during the escape that K'ola was wounded and brought to me. After everyone was relatively safe on land owned by a minor house over which the Emperor still had influence he presented the award."

There was silence in the room.

Cavahn was the first to speak. "You tell me my daughters are safe, K'ola, is she whole?" she asked firmly.

Vella looked into her mother's gaze. "She is whole, but she will not run and compete in a game of ball. She walks with a stick now. I did what I could to make it so she could run and do the things she always enjoyed...." She stopped and covered her face with her hands; sobs shook her shoulders and tears splashed on to the table as they escaped her hands. "Their spies raided the healer stations and killed all the healers and many nurse healers were also killed or wounded." Bigger floods of tears and sobs came from their third daughter.

"K'ola had returned to be with her units in the Vanguard, I was there treating her when the attack happened at my station. In one bloody hour all the other healers were dead and if it were not for me being with my sister I would also be dead." Vella took a cloth from a pocket and started drying her eyes and regaining her composure. "After the attack, I was the only healer." She looked at her hands. "I could only treat so many each day, I would work and work until I had to sleep, knowing that while I slept soldiers would die for lack of healing." She stopped and gazed at the dark space at the end of the room as if an answer was coming from it.

"One day they found me asleep on the corpse of a soldier who had died while I was treating him." She took a deep shaky breath. "K'ola's healing became complicated and I could not leave and go to her and she could not come to me. It had become too dangerous to move wounded from place to place, even at night. The Mahan and Koru attacked the separated Vanguard and Black Legion camps. If I had been able to go to her she would not walk with a stick today. She is my sister, I should have been able to take better care of her."

The NighT Guardian closed the award case and left it where it rested. "How was it to dangerous to move wounded at night? If the Vanguard has been made up to strength from lesser units, how much of what I would know is left?" His daughter looked him straight in the eye; she had expected her father to settle on issues affecting his old unit, and her mother on the health and wellness of her daughters. "They had trained Vanmor, perhaps thirty, maybe forty, we could hear them day and night, but most aggressively at night. As to what remains of the Vanguard you knew, only fifteen percent, perhaps less." Vella replied.

The answer caused the NighT Guardian to pause for a moment in confusion and loss of words. "Vanmor, they only live in the North, the North must be part of this, this rebellion. Fifteen percent is a small fraction but there must be some reserves left to restore the strength of the Vanguard."

Vella shook her head. "We never saw a northerner, we just heard the Vanmor and counted the dead the next day, anyone that made noise was dead before the next Day Rise." She sighed and looked very tired "The Emperor took the Black Legion, the Vanguard and all of their reserves into the east. It was to be a show of force at first, but then the Emperor tired of testing the strength of the Mahan and decided a short brutal campaign would settle it. But instead the Mahan and Koru ended it and humbled the

Emperor…" She waited before continuing. "Both houses have been granted Cher Sovan!"

No one said anything, Cher Sovan; the "the right hand of the Emperor" was intended to be a unique marker for houses that had supported the Emperor and Empire in dire situations. It allowed houses that had been joined together through conquest, as Mahan who had conquered Koru had, to separate and both to be treated as separate and equal Imperial Houses in the upper Senate. They were freed from taxation by the emperor but granted full taxation rights over their lands and subjects.

"The Black Legion like the Vanguard is at strength only in numbers, most are from lesser legions wearing Black Legion uniforms and juniors who had been training for entry when this happened." Vella patted her arm where her Black Legion tattoo was, "None of those from lesser legions have a Legion tattoo." Vella murmured.

Her father looked at the table and started making circles in some spilled salt as he spoke. His daughter, finally composed, answered what she expected her father wanted to hear, "There is talk of asking old members of the Legion and Vanguard to rejoin their units to give it the hard core of Legionnaires each needs should the Emperor be challenged and need his crack fighting forces."

The NighT Guardian continued making circles, now in some fresh salt he spilled just for the purpose of making circles in salt. "I could…" but he was cut off by Vella. "Father you can do nothing. I have made sure of that! I updated your medical records, you are not fit to rejoin."

"You had no right to" he barked. "If I choose to rejoin and stand side by side with others in the Vanguard I will!" He hit the table with the palm of his hand for emphasis making the spilled salt scatter across the table.

Vella leaned forward her liquid red eyes fierce and her voice cut like a knife, "Father when you stood on the front line you knew who stood to your right and left and who was behind you, you could rely on them. You had trained, lived, fought and celebrated and mourned together. You were brothers and sisters, in arms" Vella paused, "I have seen the Vanguard train many times, the sessions are brutal, long, exhausting, but they build unity and camaraderie." She slapped the table as effectively as her father. "I was present when Invar led the remaining members of the Vanguard in a training attack against the new front line."

Her eyes narrowed, "… ten percent ran away, half of those who remained shit themselves!" She sat back in her chair with a look of disgust on her face "a few even killed themselves rather than face as much as a training attack."

Vella brushed away the salt that had reached her side of the table. "I will not have my father stand on the front line and smell the shit of the man next to him, watch others run away, and hear someone behind you blow out their brains." She took a deep breath and slapped the table again, with both hands this time, she hit the table one... two... and then three times, "It is done. I made it so it cannot be undone!!" she exclaimed fiercely.

The NighT Guardian was taken aback by the strength of his daughter's demonstration.

Cavahn spoke clearly and with a level tone. "There is more, isn't there?"

Vella gathered her composure but waited to respond. "Word of what happened in the east is spreading, through the south mostly, out to the west. Of the northern houses, VodaKhan is still aligned with the Emperor, and by far the richest, the house also leads many minor northern houses who have wealth in trees, furs, winter fruits, and processed animal leather." She adjusted herself in her seat and softly continued, "I have not heard anything of my brothers, and I have discreetly enquired, but, nothing."

Cavahn rose from her seat at the head of the table and picked up the award and walked over to the side table and placed it in the centre drawer. As she closed the drawer she turned around and faced the two of them. "No matter what happened, our eldest received an award of incredible distinction and honour, which she has conferred on your father and myself." The tone of her voice was even; the words perfectly formed with no hint of her clipped western pronunciation or the rolling vowels of her order.

Vella rose and started clearing away the food warmers and the cooling trays for the deserts. Cavahn released the salt gatherer from the far end of the table where it had been silently waiting. Within a few moments while the NighT Guardian sat still thinking of the serious things they had just spoken of, the table was cleared and set for drinks and dark rich bowls of hot steeped root.

He watched Vella leave the room, walking in direction of the hallway.

Vella opened the front door and stepped outside to the edge of the Verandah where she stopped and bowed three times to the new first moon. Covering her eyes she bowed again three times. With each bow she made a small silent entreaty to her guardian spirits asking in turn for Health, Wealth, and Happiness be granted to herself and her family wherever they maybe. She walked back into the house and locked the door back to let in the cool night air and set the invisible mesh that would stop animals and people from entering. The house was not known well locally, so it was very rare that people came visiting uninvited, but animals, they could come in if chased by a predator.

As the cool night air wafted through the house it merged with the fresh sent of the steeped roots set out by Cavahn on the table. Next to the stepped root bubbling on warmer plates, a tall slender flask of pale blue western liqueur sat on a cooler plate. The coolness of the plate setting up eddies of different thicknesses and temperatures in the liquid.

Vella came back into the room bringing her healers bag. It had been a gift from her parents when she graduated and had been with her throughout her tenure in the Black

Legion. Made from animal skin by a local crafts person it now showed the wear and tear of life in the premier unit. The lock showed a heavy blow from a blunt object and odd coloured and odd shaped rivets crudely replaced those that had been there when it was new. The shoulder straps were worn and re-stitched in several places along their length. The badge of a healer had been broken in two and welded together and reattached. Some additional pouches had been added to the bag but were made of mismatched skins.

She caught her parents looking at what had been a prized gift and possession, "The life of a healer…" as if that statement answered everything. The lock still worked well and resisted the first attempt at opening it. Folding back the bag's lid and removing a couple of trays and compartments with instruments and drugs she reached down into the bottom and to one corner of the bag. One by one she took out five carefully wrapped objects, each in cloth of a different colour. Then, slowly, she replaced the trays and other parts of the bag not required and took it back to the hallway.

She paused for a moment to repeat her rituals as the first rim of second moon had just risen. This gave her father time to pour the steeped root and flavour it. He stirred the flask of liqueur breaking up the eddies and changing the strands into shorter ones that sparkled in the light of the candles and lighting globes which he turned down slightly.

Vella returned to the room and placed two of the wrapped objects to the left hand of her mother. "For my brothers, I do not know where they are or how to contact them" she said. Her mother nodded accepting them. Then Vella placed a wrapped object in front of her mother and one in front of her father. Then she sat down, one object wrapped remained in front of her.

They all took time to stop and sip the steeped root and enjoy the rich aroma and sense of quiet it brought to the family group. Then one by one, first her mother then her father opened the wrapped object to reveal a gift inside.

Cavahn exclaimed as she threw back the last fold of cloth to reveal her gift. Six gold rings, each about the size of her wrist wound around strips of leather of maroon, blue and gold. Each ring intricately decorated with designs of significant events in the sun and moon seasons. She could wear them in her hair; they would serve to keep her long hair in place and at the same time, if correctly entwined in her hair, show the season she was celebrating.

Next her father slowly unfolded the cloth surrounding his gift. When the last fold was set aside he stared dumb struck at the gift, he reached out with his left hand to stroke the gift gently and with extreme admiration. As NighT Guardian he was used to looking at each of the moons as they rose and crossed the sky above his post. He spent many hours memorizing the features that made each moon distinctive.

His gift was a strong white gold chain necklace for good fortune, health and wealth. Occasionally rocks would fall from the sky and the belief was that each moon sent a very small piece of itself to benefit those on this world. The rocks that fell possessed the same hint of colour as one of the moons. The reason the rocks fell to this world was unknown but all believed it to be for some special, mystical purpose. The part of the necklace worn at the front contained gold links coloured to match the subtle colour of each moon; into each link small disks from the fallen rocks had been crafted and added. At the back of each disk was engraved a three-word prayer, his name and his daughter who had gifted it.

The gifts given, the NighT Guardian and Cavahn joined hands and bowed their heads to their daughter who returned the bow. No words of thanks were said; a gift freely given and gratefully received does not require words, so none was said.

Vella poured a small bowl of the liqueur and sipped on it. She did not look at the small wrapped package in front of her. Her parents waited. She finished the liqueur and set the bowl aside.

"And then there is this." Slowly and with some reverence she unwrapped the object. Finally, she finished. She put the object aside and straightened the cloth and placed the object back in the centre of the cloth with some reverence.

Her mother inhaled deeply and breathed out slowly, "I have only heard of those, I have never seen one, is it what I think it is?" Vella nodded. The NighT Guardian rose and walked around to be beside his daughter and looked down at the object in the centre of the cloth, he nodded and sat down.

It was a Fan Book.

Fan Books came from a time when the ability to read was confined to royalty and very wealthy, before the time of printing on paper and reading tablets, there were Fan Books. The very first were made from root pulp but only a very, very few survived from that era. Then the books were made from wood, and then wood pulp. With each change in material, the ability to make more books and share them grew. But still, it is the books made from metal that had lasted the longest and were the most prized.

A Fan Book works rather like the crescents ladies at court unfolded and used to move air over their faces to keep them cool, or simply to hide part or all of their face. Instead of being used to move air; you unfolded each section of a Fan Book to read what is written there, then you moved to the next section and so on. Some Fan Books were quite large both in size and the number of sections. There were special desks on which large Fan Books could be placed and read. This one was very small and easily carried.

"It is…" Vella said and then paused, "…a simple book on the healing of cuts in children. I bought it because it relates to healing." Vella stopped to look at her parents and to pour another small bowl of liqueur; she sipped from it and set it down. "There is nothing in it I do not know, it is just very valuable, and very, very collectable. The seller said it was from the Fourth Imperial Period." She rolled the Fan Book over carefully and indicated some markings at the back at bottom of the Fan Book. "I have verified the markings, they are from the middle of that period." She stopped to take another sip from the bowl.

"How could you afford such a rare object?" Her mother was curious at her daughter's apparent great wealth. The gifts she and the NighT Guardian had received were far from insignificant and she could only imagine the gifts her daughter was leaving for her brothers were of equal quality.

"I was asked by a senior officer to help heal the daughter of a wealthy eastern merchant and senate member. As a gift, the merchant allowed me to buy all these gifts and the book and only pay what I could afford, a pittance of what they are worth. The officer issued a waver based on the value I paid, not the value of the items. The amount I paid was so low that it need not be declared as transmission of wealth between a political officer and senator, and myself from the military."

Her mother leant forward, "But the officer who asked you to carry out the healing would have benefited in someway!

Vella nodded, "I am sure he did for the short period he was alive. He was killed the day following his recording the transaction. I also recorded the gift being given, the exchange of money such as it was, and the reason for it." With that said, her mother leaned back smiling. "Yes, it is valuable because of its age, and what it is, but the subject is not attractive, politics, romance and pornography are much more sought after." Vella nodded but didn't seem to care, "This is what is interesting."

She turned the book over once again, "Each book bears the emblem of the house for which it was created. This book is from the era when books were only made for a noble house, and the book had to recorded in the Imperial archive." She looked at her parents in turn. "Books were knowledge back then, knowledge had to be controlled and the Imperial family thought that by recording books they could keep a record of who possessed what knowledge. The marks above the house emblem are the author, the bookmaker, the Imperial Archivist and year the book was entered in the Archives. The bookmaker was bound by law to send the book to be recorded in the archive and pay the appropriate taxes before giving it to the owner."

With the small finger of her right hand she indicated a series of small symbols hammered into the back of the Fan Book at the bottom corner. Then carefully she opened the book a little, like an insect emerging from its cocoon twenty or so sections of a fan appeared. She indicated the same symbols on each section. Then she placed the partly opened book in the cloth and slid the cloth and book to her mother. "Each section has the same symbols as on the back. Plus, there is a special symbol added by the Imperial Archivist. That symbol is a code that marks each section within the book as unique."

Her mother stared at the symbols on the back cover and on each section. "So if a section was removed or a section added anyone looking at the book would know immediately?" She looked at her daughter for confirmation.

"Yes. They were more worried about sections being removed and given to others. In that way knowledge could be spread and Imperial control lost. There was also the issue of taxation. A secondary way to control the dispersal of knowledge and books was to tax the number of sections in a book, as well as its size and weight. If a section were added or the size and weight of the book did not agree with the code stamps, it was likely the correct taxes had not been paid."

Her mother nodded. If there was two things the Imperial family was good at it was control and taxation. "I don't recognize the house symbol." She looked up at Vella, "House Vernanco" her daughter provided. "The house disappeared a hundred years after the book was entered in the Archives. I checked the history records, when House Karrep-et destroyed Vernanco one prince and two princesses were married into Karrep-et, the rest of House Vernanco nobles and family members were slaughtered, close to four hundred met their death in an orgy of executions over three days."

Her mother turned the book up slightly so that she could see the individual sections of the Fan Book. Each section did indeed bear consistent markings. In addition to the markings on the back, the Imperial Archivist had added their personal, unique, code mark to each section. The mark with the others made each section unique within the book, and reinforced the uniqueness of the book. Also, it was completely certain that nothing could be removed or added without the Imperial marks becoming inconsistent, the book was, and always would be original and complete.

Cavahn turned the cloth with the book the right way up and slid it across the table to the NighT Guardian who turned to a wall case behind him and took from it a magnifier and started to study the marks on the back and each section.

He sat up and looked at each of them in turn. "What you just said does not make sense. A hundred years after House Vernanco was destroyed and the family executed they commissioned a book and the Imperial Archivist knowingly recorded it in the archives. Have you checked the imperial Archives for the book?" He asked.

Vella licked the rim of her liqueur bowl and then took a sip. "Yes I have. It was recorded correctly and the initials of who made the entry were none other than the Imperial Archivist in office at the time. It was not an official or attendant of the archivist office that made the entry. The book was recorded in the first quarter of the year, the Archivist's office was hardly overworked, they had one hundred and forty nine other officials or attendants and recorded just four hundred and six books in that period. Less than 3 books per attendant in that quarter of the year."

Her mother spoke to her daughter while watching her husband carefully scrutinize the book. "That sounds impossible. The Archivist should have reported the bookmarker and the person commissioning the book to the Imperial Supervisors. The Supervisors would arrest them and if necessary prosecute and execute them after extracting whatever information they could."

"I could not find any information on who commissioned the book, but the bookmaker lived a long happy life after registering that book and he produced many, many more during his life time." She said rather sleepily as the Liqueur started to take effect.

"And… so, Vella, what do you expect us to do with this?" Her mother asked.

Her daughter responded but not with an answer to her question. "Here's the thing, during his life time that particular bookmaker registered another ten books commissioned by House Vernanco and there were four other books commissioned by the same house and made by three other bookmakers."

Her daughter put down her liqueur bowl and rested her head on the back of the high back chair she was sitting in as if she wanted to go to bed and sleep. "Please keep it for me." After a moment she yawned and abruptly pushed her chair back and shakily stood up. She was drunk. She picked up the bowl and liqueur flask and walked out of the living room in the direction of the stairs to the upper level and her room.

The NighT Guardian looked at Cavahn who was sitting very relaxed in her chair. Then her expression changed to one of distaste. She brought the back of her right hand up to cover her mouth, the first two fingers extended and the little finger and thumb touching across the palm of her hand, she burped. "Too much spice in the third course!" she said.

The NighT Guardian rose from the table and walked to a small wall case at the end of the room and took out a flask of liqueur and brought it back to place it on the vacant cooler plate. This flask contained a blue greenish liqueur, the cooler plate started to generate thick swirls of colour in the fluid. While the cooler plate did its work, he carefully closed the book and wrapped it in its cloth.

She looked at him, "I take it the liqueur our daughter got drunk on was…"

"The cheap stuff" he interrupted watching the swirls in the fluid reach the top of the flask. Cavahn pushed her bowl towards him. He filled it, then his own and placed the flask back on the cooler plate.
"So it seams this has been going on for hundreds of years and even imperial officials have known." He said first smelling the fragrant scent of the premium liqueur in his bowl and then sipping it gently.

"Let's just get drunk, like our daughter?" Cavahn held out her bowl to The NighT Guardian who in turn held his bowl out to her. The bowls gently touched and first she and then he poured a small quantity of liqueur from their bowl into the other; it was an intimate act of sharing and agreement.

The NighT Guardian opened an eye to see what was rocking the hammock bed so much.

Cavahn had risen and the change in weight on her side of the hammock had caused the swaying of the bed. He lazily moved to the centre of the bed to adjust its weight and slow and then stop the swinging motion.

Soon after they had come home from the west, outside on the second level verandah, he had built a hammock bed equally as palatial and comfortable as the master bed in their bedroom that opened on to the verandah a few feet away. They had the option of sleeping inside or out, if outside on the hammock bed they could better enjoy the cool breezes from the river. The hammock bed would sway back and forth pushed gently by their sleep, their love making, or just by the breezes.

Through his one eye he could tell that First Sun must be half risen. The liqueur and his desire for more rest sent him back to sleep.

Cavahn looked back over her shoulder at the NighT Guardian. Since she had risen, as she knew he would, he had moved to the centre of the bed, she watched his tongue lick his lips and catch a small amount of drool trying to escape the corner of his mouth. He was already asleep as she turned to walk through the door into their master bedroom.

She had heard muffled voices from down stairs; she recognized Vella's voice and another she had not heard for a couple of years now, the fancied it was Lovan, their second son. She stopped at the large mirror and brushed her hair without much conviction. And moved on quickly.

She passed by Vella's bedroom. It was a mess. The bed coverings were on the floor at the foot of the bed as was one of the pillows. The other was at a crazy angle at the top of the bed. The flask her daughter had taken to bed with her was empty and on its side on the floor as was the sipping bowl. The bowl was upturned with a stain all around it. It must have been full before being upturned. Clothes were strewn around the room. Her travel bags lay open with the contents partly thrown on the floor.

Cavahn knew Vella's boots were still at the front door with all the others in the house. However, Vella's house shoes lay in the middle of the hallway leading to the stairs. Cavahn picked them up and set them side by side next to the door to her daughter's room. A chore she had carried out almost daily for many years until her daughter had left for school to be a healer.

As Cavahn moved down the stairs she passed the passage to the kitchen, and her senses were overwhelmed by the warm comforting smell of food baking in the stove and pots simmering on the top burners. Vella might have been drunk last night, but she had been up early and prepared a very tasty breakfast if the smells were any indication.

The dinning room was as she and the NighT Guardian left it. The front door was open still but the invisible mesh was turned off. Cavahn walked out on to the verandah to see a military issue-sleeping roll at the right side of the door; its cover open and the head roll still showing the indentation of the sleeper's head. Second son, Lovan, had returned home during the night found the door open, but the invisible force mesh engaged preventing him from entering. He had slept in his sleeping roll by the door.

She was surprised to feel the hand of the NighT Guardian on her hip; she felt her body lean back slightly and press up against him. She looked over her left shoulder and smiled at the bleary eyed Guardian. He stood there naked, idly fingering his navel. "I could not sleep with all this noise!"

Cavahn patted his face and spoke quietly. "We would not have left you out of a family shower." She turned and walked to the large shower at the far right end of the verandah. As she walked she dropped her rob and was naked by the time she reached the shower. Cooling water from the river was pumped through pipes many feet underground to preserve the water's perfect temperature.

Vella and Lovan were already enjoying relaxing in an invigorating shower, and seeing their parents joining them, they called out their appreciation and jibes at how long it had taken them to wake from last nights drunken events.

In the shower they all took turns hugging Lovan as the water poured over them and ran off to the vegetable plantings along the side of the hill into which the house was built.

Vella and Lovan took large drying cloths that completely enwrapped them head to foot and walked off towards a table at the other end of the verandah. At the front door, Vella went in to the house to check on her breakfast cooking in the kitchen.

Cavahn picked up the sponge and beckoned the NighT Guardian to turn around so she could soap his body and carefully started washing it as if she were washing away the injuries she saw on his body. There were scars and puncture wounds over much of his body. Each had its own history like the one caused by a spear thrust upwards by a drying enemy that entered his back and glanced off the NighT Guardian's shoulder blade and exited his body at the right shoulder. He had turned and slain the enemy on the ground but needed a fellow member of the Vanguard to extract the spear from his body.

Cavahn handed the NighT Guardian the soap and soaping cloth and looked him in the eye "This is becoming quite the family reunion" she whispered. He took the soaping cloth and applied more soap to it. Cavahn turned around and rested her arms on a shelf in the shower. Before he applied the soaping cloth the NighT Guardian ran his hands over her slim back. Her always-tanned skin had been tattooed from shoulder to the dimples above her buttocks. Elaborate angelic wings had been tattooed in white ink as a contrast to her tanned skin colour.

The ink once injected under the skin thickened and caused the skin to rise up forming ridges of intricate flowing design under the skin. The effect was of three-dimensional white wings that appeared would grow out of her back and allow her to fly away. He always marveled at this combination of effects. Only those in the west could preform this type of tattooing and they guarded the secrete of how to formulate the ink and inject it under the skin so that it would both raise the skin and colour it as the same time. Such elaborate tattoos were both a picture and a touchable sensation. He kissed her back between her shoulder blades where it appeared the wings were attached to her body. He then applied soap and then water to wash her from head to foot.

Cavahn turned and kissed him and turned off the water. She handed him a drying cloth and taking one for her self, they wrapped themselves completely in the thick material and walked along the verandah to join Lovan.

Lovan was tall like his mother but had the musculature of his father. He had the thick long hair of his mother but his was much darker, he had the same liquid red eyes as Cavahn. While there was no doubt that Lovan was in imperial service, he had never said exactly what he did. The NighT Guardian had concluded that Lovan was involved in clandestine work of some sort and was always a little confused as to why such an easily identifiable person should be chosen for such work.

There was no formality at the breakfast table, not in this family! Vella was in the kitchen removing the baked and simmering breakfast from the stove and preparing the cart to bring food and drinks to the table.

When Vella appeared with the breakfast cart and set out the containers of hot and cold breakfast food and the appropriate nutritional drinks for each course many commendations and happy statements about the quality and volume of the prepared breakfast feast were expressed by all.

After the meal had been set out and Vella was seated, Lovan held up his left hand with the traditional index finger and thumb extended, the remaining fingers were folded against his hand. In this way the finger and thumb appeared like the vowel "L", but it also meant that all who saw the sign should listen acutely because a message was to be delivered and the message will be said once only. Around the table, silence fell allowing the reedbirds and the insects they live off to be heard clearly from down by the river.

With a very flat, matter of fact tone, and without any pre warning as to the nature of the message, Lovan made the announcement that Callar, Lovan's older brother, his parent's first son, was dead. Callar had been in the North; the details of how he met his end were unclear. It is probable he had been killed by or for House VodaKhan preventing his discoveries about them being carried back to the Senate.

There was no exclamation from either parent or sister; the announcement was greeted with no change in the stillness and silence around the table. They would each mourn the loss of their child or brother in their own time and in their own way. Mourning was a special personal thing, although they were together, now, at the table, they would not mark Callar's passing. They were not like those who came together in elaborate funerals and remembrances of a past life and the freeing of the persons soul and guardian spirits from a physical form. To those around the table, the physical body had ended its existence. While it existed, the body had been a container, a vehicle, a means for the spirit it contained to learn and grow, the spirit that was Callar had returned to its own existence and it would live again in another physical form where it would learn and acquire new experiences, and enrich other lives the bidy came into contact with.

For several minutes after Lovan made his announcement they sat quietly, some like the NighT Guardian were already reaching back into their memories about Callar. The NighT Guardian recalled the times down by the river when they had been swimming or fishing. How they had staid out under the stars reading books and stories of adventure by the moons as they rose and set. How his first son had problems with tests and assessments set by his Educator. The NighT Guardian had often completed them for Callar; the Educator had discovered this and called the NighT Guardian to his son's class where he humbled the NighT Guardian, not Callar in front of the students.

Cavahn thought of the ecstasy of childbirth, when they had arrived at this house from the west birth was the first feminine thing she stamped on this building to make it their home. It was she and she alone that made this building, handed down to the NighT Guardian by his father and mother, uniquely theirs by giving birth on the verandah above them under the light of second moon to their first daughter and eventually to Callar.

The warmth and wonder in the uniquely simple, joyous act of birthing gave her the root of pride and honour in Callar. As he grew and was educated he gained accomplishments and set and achieved goals that brought him to manhood. His spirit grew and soared with these successes, successes that would eventually take him in to the military and rapidly into Imperial service, where he became an interpreter and eventually was dispatched to the place where he ultimately met his end.

Vella turned her chair around so that her back was facing the table and the others and watched the reeds sway in the breeze and the small scurrying animals moving in and out of them on the ground. It was there that Callar had saved her from the monster that lived in the reeds and preyed on young girls. He had then staid up with her reading comforting stories until first day rise, then she had fallen asleep and he had gone to his educator, tired but satisfied that his young sister was safe from the monster in the reeds.

When Vella turned her chair back to face the table, she started to serve breakfast.

Silence.

Even the sound of the feeding utensils on the bright ceramic breakfast plates was muted. Breakfast continued at a slow pace, not because of what had been said, what it meant for each of them or how they would each come to terms with the change Callar's death brought, but because at the end of the meal, the last course while it was brought to the table steaming hot had cooled and was eaten almost cold to be at its best.

At the end of the meal Cavahn raised her right hand to her forehead, with two fingers covering her eyes she waited for the other's to do the same. When all had their eyes and fingers in a similar position she dropped her hand. Her eyes remained closed for a moment as she remained in silent gratitude and appreciation for what they had consumed and the fellowship of family members.

The hand at the forehead symbolized the concentration of thought and focus of the third, spiritual eye, the fingers over the eyes, the denial of physical vision as gratitude was expressed spiritually in a non-verbal way. The fingers over the eyes also served to remove one of the senses allowing a more complete moment of peace and inner calm to come over each of them.

Vella rose and pulled the plates to her side of the table and then placed each on the grass in front of the verandah. At the edge of the reeds there was a noticeable gathering of small furry creatures, eyes intent on her actions. This was the family's gift to the animals; the animals crossed the grass between the reeds and the house cautiously but with growing confidence until they reached the plates. They started to clean the plates using their sharp biting teeth to scratch off dried food and bite into pieces of left overs on the plates.

At the table they watched silently as the animals fed. One by one, the animals left the plates and scampered across the grass to the coolness of the reeds and the water. The last one left by the plates stood on his hind legs, brought his powerful front paws together as if clenched in prayer and bowed. The NighT Guardian stood, gathered his fits together in tight balls and looked at the furry creature and bowed his head, returning the acknowledgment. For a moment his eyes met the black round eyes of the furry creature, in this shared moment there was an exchange of recognition and observance. Then the creature was gone, scampering across the grass to join the others that waited for him at the edge of the reeds.

Lovan looked at the cloth in front of him containing his gift. Vella had set it out for him with his breakfast bowls. He toyed with the edge of the cloth, rolling the gold braided edge back and forth in his fingers. He shifted on his seat in the silence at the table.

"Open it!" The command from Vella was that of an officer to a recruit, a master to a servant, and it demanded immediate action.

Stung by the authority of her command Lovan flipped open the triangular amber cloth until sitting in the centre was his gift. A singularly beautiful, small, compact "spy" glass, exceptionally crafted and capable of clear, long distance vision, the sort used by senior officers on the battle field as they followed the action of their units. It was highly unlikely the high-ranking officer who had owned it gave it up willingly! At the front end of the spyglass, the raised emblem of House Koru was clearly mounted. Vella explained that Invar had acquired it on one of her missions behind Koru lines, and had passed it to her to deliver to Lovan as a gift.

The NighT Guardian, reached over and took the spyglass from the cloth in front of Lovan and admired it, but looking at Vella he stated the obvious. "Koru is not just pressing soldiers into the field, they are manufacturing all the tools, accouterments and accessories of war." Rolling the spyglass in his hands, he looked at Lovan, "This officer's accessory is made for show and decoration as well as function, it is made for a noble, and a simple soldier would have nothing like this to do the same job. Koru is not dead, not assimilated, is it?"

Cavahn, seeing the spyglass rose from her seat and went inside. She returned carrying the cloth containing the Fan Book and laid it on the table. Carefully Cavahn opened the cloth and took out the Fan Book and opened it fully. Seeing this, Vella shifted in her chair so as to both look at the fully open book and Lovan more clearly.

Taking her seat, Cavahn met Lovan's gaze. Absolute silence existed over the table and all around it. The sort of silence that only questions seeking answers from someone who knows the solution but may not provide it can create. Slowly, carefully, and with occasional confirmation from Vella, Cavahn one by one described the significance of the markings as well as the hidden meaning behind them. Vella and Cavahn see in Lovan someone watching and listening to what is described about the Fan Book but is detached, as if they are checking of a list but keeping the list concealed.

As Cavahn and Vella finish Lovan looks transfixed at the book and makes no response to his mother or his sister, he does not move, he simply continues to look at the book and then the spyglass; he looks in the direction of a buzzing noise to his left. It is now full Mid Day Rise, that time of day when first and second sun are at right angels to each other in the sky as if one is pulling the other back from setting and the other is being pulled into full height overhead in the sky. The twin suns will remain in that dynamic tension for several hours. It is already extremely, extremely hot for anyone without the shade of a verandah or a house partially covered by a small hill. Down by the reeds, the small furry creatures are not to be seen, they will be down by the water, in the water, or in their small reed nests that completely cover them.

On the prison wall, the Day Guardians will stand watch, their cloaks completely covering them now, nothing, not even a finger will be exposed.

The buzzing sound grows louder. The sound comes from a plant rich in beautiful colours, branches and leaves, it is rich in water. As the heat of Mid Day Rise boils the water in its branches, it recycles the steam back into its deep roots where it is cool and the moist steam condenses back into water. As water it will rise back up into the branches of the plant carrying with it added nutrients from the ground soil that will help the plant grow. Once the nutrients have been absorbed the water will boil again and be recycled back into the deep roots and so the cycle repeat over and over during the day. The movement of water and steam inside the plant create a buzzing sound as the cycle of water and steam, steam and water repeat over and over.

Lovan turns his face back to his family. He draws the cloth with the Fan Book to him and picks up the book and studies the markings for barely a couple of seconds and then closes the book and places it back on the cloth. Slowly and carefully, he wraps the book and pushes it back to Cavahn.

Looking at his father, "No doubt father, as Senior NighT Guardian and first beneficiary of the Layer's from the executed, you have other examples." It was a statement, not a question. "This has been happening for centuries, not years, not decades." Lovan paused. "I am sure you know that when books were restricted, when you could not make them, or have them made, own or sell them without reporting to the Imperial Archivist to have an unregistered book was a serious crime." Lovan looked at the cloth package on the table in front of his mother, "It was not so much that wealthy houses could afford to commission books and pay taxes on them, or the knowledge the books contained. The Imperial Family thought they could control knowledge it by controlling ownership and movement of books. The Archivist was one source of information about how the houses were using their wealth and the knowledge they were gathering and recording in books. The real issue was that some of the houses were spending large sums on books and building libraries rather than building roads, bridges, and stage camps to make it easy for the Emperor to move troops around the empire." Lovan looked down at his drying cloth and picked at a loose thread.

As Lovan started to wrap the spyglass carefully in its amber clothe. "Do you know how many there are in the Imperial family now, how much land they have and the castles they have built? The life style they live?" He looked around his family as if the answer could be found amongst them. "No answer! Well, there is no shame in it." He opened his body cloth a little to let out some of his own steam. "House VodaKhan in the North." He paused to look at the spyglass. "The Imperial family long ago outstripped what can be gathered by taxation and levies. The violence and revolts of the Fifth Imperial Period over taxation were settled by a secret pact between VodaKhan and the Emperor. VodaKhan seized the initiative to supply gold to the Imperial family; in return the Imperials reduced their taxes and levies ending the violence. To cement the deal VodaKhan was and always has provided unyielding support for the Emperor in the Senate, doing so has given them secret access to Emperors plans. The Emperor turns a blind eye to anything regarding the activities of House VodaKhan."

"NighT Guardian!" Lovan addressed his father by title rather than by name. "The campaign in the west where you met mother, do you know the real reason for it?"

The NighT Guardian shrugged his shoulders. It was a long time ago, they had raised an entire family since he had returned from the west.

"Sailing ships owned by the western families returning across the Great Salt Sea sail north and stop at secret VodaKhan ports in the far north." Lovan took a sip of river liquid before continuing, "In those ports they take on VodaKhan gold destined for the Imperial Family and then the ships head south to their homeports. The gold is secretly offloaded with the other cargo. Taxes are paid only on the visible cargo, not the gold hidden in it."

Lovan now poured himself a large glass of chilled river liquid and drank at it thirstily before continuing. "The western families take a percentage of the smuggled gold and let the goods, Imperial taxes and hidden gold continue to the Imperial Family, the gold is removed and stored in castles such as the one you guard now and call a prison." Lovan waited for his father to react.

"I have always thought of it as a castle where a prison exists and the Emperor changes it from a castle to a prison and back depending on whether he holds court there?" responded the NighT Guardian.

"Yes, father, you are correct, the Emperor does hold court there from time to time and then it is called a castle. But for most for the year it is a prison. When it is a prison a senior member of the family trusted by the emperor is in charge. In reality it is a major gold store. If you look at the senior members of the Imperial Family, there are 20 of them, they all live at prisons while much lesser members live in castles. Have you not found that strange?"

Lovan looked at his father with great concentration. "The Emperor went to war with the western families because he felt they were taking too much gold from each shipment, he wanted to stop it and take all they had accumulated for himself. If he could seize the gold stores of each house he reasoned he could become independent of the VodaKhan's and break the western families at the same time. Ever since the Imperial family made their pact with VodaKhan they have chaffed at it and tried to break its hold over them. In the west it was not the western houses taking too much from each shipment; it was VodaKhan shipping small amounts. Their gold mines were exhausted and new mines had yet to be proven. Do you know why you left the west so quickly father?" Lovan asked.

The NighT Guardian shrugged his shoulders. "It was because the first elements, those that attack behind the Vanguard came down with a great illness and the Emperor decided he did not want to waste weakened troops against stronger opponents. Other than that, no, it was a long time ago, I don't remember." The NighT Guardian returned Lovan's challenging gaze, "I suppose you have the answer?"

"Yes, I do!" Lovan continued sipping at his bowl. "It is true there was a great illness, many died from it but the western armies proved stronger than the Emperor expected. However, the real reason you left the west so quickly was because the western houses sent their gold stores north and warned their ships to stay in the northern ports. VodaKhan also warned the Emperor that to press his attack would result in no more gold, ever."

The NighT Guardian sat still, thinking for a long moment. "So that would be why we never attacked the rich coastal cities that had little in the way of defense though it was well within our ability to take the cities even with weakened forces and bend them to the Emperor's banner." He looked at Cavahn, "We could not attack them because they were the homeports for the ships bringing the gold down from the north. The ships would never have returned if the Emperor's banner was flying over the cities."

Lovan put his feet up on the table footrest and lounged back in his chair. He had their attention and enjoyed divulging his knowledge of the secrets of power that made their world turn "The Emperor's adventures in the west disrupted many things. He was forced to make another significant deal with VodaKhan and the western families this time. As mines were proven gold shipments increased in frequency and size but the western houses were allowed to increase their share of what passed through their ports and lands; in the Senate they created voting blocks that could keep fully one third of the Senate neutral. With one third of the Senate always neutral, they could frustrate the Emperor quiet easily on any issue of importance. House VodaKhan would continue to publicly support the Imperial Family as they had always done but in return, the Imperial family now was not to advance troops anywhere VodaKhan didn't want them to go."

Lovan ran his fingers through his long hair. "The submission and assimilation of houses by more powerful ones secretly stopped some time after the Fifth Imperial Period, our tradition of one house absorbing another is a fiction and the execution of nobles in the lesser houses also stopped around that time. Which is why trinkets show up proclaiming the smaller house within a larger house. Members of the lesser house commission them."

The NighT Guardian interrupted his son, "But there are less seats in the senate than there used to be. The seats of assimilated houses have passed to those who they integrated with. Where have those seats gone?"

"There are fewer "House Seats" which is historically where the power lay, but have you counted the number of administrative, judicial, and trade sponsored seats that have appeared? There is greater potential to ferment political action in the senate if VodaKhan wants because those seats are not aligned to land, region or historical accident."

"The attack in the east against Mahan was… "

"A trap. The Emperor thought he saw evidence he could use to bring the non-aligned houses to his side and also wage war on VodaKhan. He hoped to capture and control their gold mines by going to the East and then North. If he could achieve that, the Imperial Family would again become the ultimate power."

"So that is why there were Vanmor and their handlers from the North!" Vella exclaimed, "and Koru troops from the Far East, so well supplied, and moving so fast." She adopted a pose of great thoughtfulness. "The haste of the Vanguard and the Black Legion's advance… the way they became separated…" Vella's voice trailed off, she was starting to realize that the failure and decimation of the two great fighting forces was planned, not an accident.

"Actually" Lovan looked earnestly at her, "The Emperor is not a bad tactician, perhaps if he had gone to the east all those years ago, instead of west he might have made more progress or even succeeded. But if he had done that, mother would not have met father and we would not be here!"

"The Emperor had to find a way to try and bring the Imperial family out from under the influence of VodaKhan, but the house has agents everywhere, especially the military. The house knew what the emperor was planning long before the legion broke camp and misguided and misinformed him."

"What about today and tomorrow?" Questioned the NighT Guardian.

"The noose around the Imperial Family and especially the Emperor was set a longtime ago. VodaKhan has tugged on it from time to time to bring the Emperor back into line when he has strayed, and they manipulate the Senate artfully from behind the scenes. With this misadventure in the east, it has been pulled tight."

In the clarity of the day and remembering what had been said the NighT before, the NighT Guardian sat, hands clasped, rotating his thumbs around each other in contemplation. "VodaKhan have achieved what they wanted, the Emperor is weakened and the strongest and best legions have been destroyed. They will never allow them to regroup or be any military threat to them."

The NighT Guardian lounged back in his chair, his words said, the flavour of the changes coming to his world, all their worlds, was apparent. He listened to the buzzing of the water moving in the plants near by and rhythm of the river Ohm in the distance. The reality was and is that his family was aware of great changes happening but with little ability to influence them and for people like the boot maker in the village, what happened to the powerful was of little importance so long as their lives and spirits continued.

Without realizing it, he started to snooze.

The others drifted into their own silent contemplative spaces. A cool breeze from the river drifted up and under the verandah ceiling where it was held for a while before escaping at each end only to loose its coolness to the fierce head of full day rise. The buzzing sound from the plants continued to lull all around the table.

Crack!

The sound of a heavy boot against the wood of the verandah floor, it was startling, and very necessary.

They had a guest they had been ignoring.

Rather incautiously all turned in their chairs and looked at the neglected guest.

A tall slender girl stood on the grass at the edge of the verandah. She was almost the same height as Lovan who was taller than the NighT Guardian, but slightly shorter than Cavahn. She wore a very broad round black hat with a stove pipe top, except the stove pipe was not round, it was square, a clear marker she was from the south west, the far south west, much, much further than the NighT Guardian had been when he met his spouse.

She did not wear the heavy cloaks usually found in this part of the world to protect against the heat of full Day Rise. Like the first time the NighT Guardian met Cavahn, the girl was wearing a long Maroon dress with matching maroon cape edged with purple and gold braided rope. Her eyes were the same red liquid as those of Cavahn but a deeper red, only a shade lighter than the colour of the maroon cloak. On the floor beside her boots, very heavy boots, boots intended to be worn for travel that lasted weeks, not days, rested a neatly folded bed roll bound to a travel backpack with purple and gold braided rope. At her waist, attached to a belt made of the same purple and gold braided rope, a black knife, maybe the length of the NighT Guardian's forearm and accented with gold was securely attached.

The size and heft of the knife and her appearance and demeanor told the NighT Guardian, this person knew how to wield the knife and was not scared to display it openly. Surprised and slightly confused at the fact he had obviously fallen asleep and his senses so dulled by rest and good food that her approach had not woken him, the NighT Guardian … farted!

The act of expelling intestinal gas caused everyone at the table and the guest to turn their attention to him. "Sorry!" The NighT Guardian exclaimed. "Too much baked sun plant and roots for breakfast" the NighT Guardian tried to find any excuse for the odor he had created he started waving his arms and drying cloth vigorously to disperse it.

Vella turned in her chair from looking at their guest to stare cold-eyed at the NighT Guardian, "Really, I had to bake extra for you, knowing your thirst for that dish, we would have had none to share if not for that extra work early this morning."

Lovan opened his mouth as if to speak but the NighT Guardian's spouse raised her left hand; the small finger extended over the palm of her hand to meet her thumb.

Silence.

Although Cavahn was still wearing nothing but her large drying cloth, her presence expanded beyond the verandah. She turned to their guest, "Step up on to the verandah floor and come out of the heat of Day Rise. Bring your pack. Remove your boots, your hat. As you do these things, you enter my domain." Cavahn paused. "In my domain, I rule absolutely!" She paused before continuing. "If you do not obey me, I will expel you with a brutality you will not witness again because you will be dead. Do you understand?"

Around the table, all were aware their mother had a "presence" but it had been firm and gentle in its application as they grew from babies to adults, it had resulted in a beautifully ordered and happy home. As Cavahn had turned to speak to their guest part of her drying cloth had fallen from her shoulder revealing part of one of the raised white wing tattoos on her back.

Lovan focused on the part of the raised tattoo he could see. For all his life the family had enjoyed the outdoor family showers and they had become forgetful of the intricate, white, raised wing tattoos that covered his mother's back.

The guest clasped her hands together in tight balls and pressed them together in front her. She did not look down at her balled hands as was common, she looked intently into Cavahn's eyes. As she did, she stepped onto the verandah floor and out of the Day Rise heat and brightness. She stood there, and she looked down at her hands. "Winged Angel! I am in your domain, I am subject to you in all ways." After a moment's pause she reached back and brought her pack onto the verandah beside her and then removed her boots as instructed. She turned to look at Cavahn who indicated a vacant chair at the table.

Cavahn met Vella's gaze, "Please, breakfast for the supplicant. And river liquid, I am sure our guest is thirsty." At this, the girl sat where Cavahn had indicated and removed her hat and placed it on the floor. She waited patiently.

Cavahn rose from her chair and moved easily with the drying clothe around her to the entrance of the house. The NighT Guardian however was not so gracious. As he rose from his chair the drying cloth started to fall and he hastily clasped it to him and at the same time, he tried with obvious difficulty to hand sign to Lovan that he should remain at the table with the guest. She was not to be left alone. Lovan responded with the appropriate signal that he understood.

As the NighT Guardian walked towards the door of the house, he was forced to gather the drying cloth up from dragging on the floor in a large untidy ream so that his legs just above the knee were revealed and his upper torso, he walked awkwardly toward the door, desperately trying to prevent it from falling all the way down. When he was inside the door and out of sight of the breakfast table, the NighT Guardian simply dropped the entire clothe to the floor, and stood naked gathering it in to a large ball of material and walked briskly to catch up to Cavahn.

At the entrance to their bedroom he gazed at Cavahn's naked back and the intricate white tattoo and the subtle effect of the raised skin. Standing several feet away he could almost see real wings attached to Cavahn's back that may extend at any moment and sweep her out through the open verandah doors and into the sky.

He walked up to her and gently ran his fingers across the tattoo. "I never thought how special you are! I mean, not in the way our guest referred to you," he said softly so they were not heard downstairs. Cavahn looked over her left shoulder at him and smiled. She took his chin in her left hand and kissed him. "WE…" she said with an emphasis she reserved for the deepest and strongest messages, "… are lovers. In this life, our spirits are excellent lovers and that is what matters. The wings come from a time when I was chosen for a role in my order by people that did not care whether I wanted it or not. In this life my spirit is here to learn, to blend a wife, lover, mother, parent, and things I don't know about yet. What I I learn will help me in the next life." She dropped the drying cloth and walked naked to the closet.

The full height of Day Rise had stilled the air outside the cool shade of the lower verandah. The NighT Guardian stepped bare footed on to the cool wood floor. Simple black trousers caught at the waist with a plain belt of black animal skin taken and cured long ago from a Vanmor, A yellow buckle with the crest of the Vanguard in Gold and a black shirt with the yellow emblem of the Senior NighT Guardian on its collar lay open at the neck.

Cavahn followed him out a few moments later, the clothing, the delay between their appearance and the affirmation of their organization and stature had been carefully discussed and planned in their bedroom.

Cavahn, also barefoot but wearing a luxurious maroon dress with blue and gold rope piping, at her waist an intricately woven belt where the same blue and gold intertwined and played against each other in an intricate design. The dress flowed to the floor in straight narrow and broad pleats, similar to the one she wore when the NighT Guardian first met her, however this dress had a high collar that framed Cavahn's red tinged hair and vibrant face. On the outside of the collar intricate blue and gold designs indicated her status in her order. Mysteriously, she had never described the role to the Night Guardian who had accepted simply that it was "special".

For a moment Cavahn turned to look out over the grass and reeds shimmering in the heat of Full Day Rise, as she did the dress is revealed to be backless, the NighT Guardian had always thought of the dress, as sexually stimulating and Cavahn knew it. It had been worn several times for that reason.

But now the true reason for the backless dress was clear. The dark maroon of the dress appeared as a picture frame clearly highlighting the intricate white wing design under her tanned skin.

At Cavahn's waist, a knife, similar to the black blade worn by the girl, but the blade is a milky blue and had been freely exhibited it in a special display in their bedroom. The knife sheath is disarmingly simple. It is simple hammered metal, the sort a soldier on the line would use for their blade. It is embellished with simple stones from the Great Salt Sea in a design depicting the three moons as in K'ola's award Vella presented to them the night before.

Cavahn had let the NighT Guardian hold her blade the first time she had set it out for display. He had marveled at the balance of the knife, it was perfect for slashing, thrusting and stabbing motions, and he could see that it was an exact fit for his spouse's knife hand. Once in her hand the blade would remain firmly planted, it would not twist or rotate in combat. It would become an extension of the arm that wielded it but its colour was an oddity, a curiosity.

The knife was clearly designed for combat; to be used by someone trained to use it, use it to kill. He had always seen the knife as being designed for such a purpose but for some reason unknown to him, he had never spoken of it or asked why Cavahn would possess such a knife. That first time she let him hold it, he had merely touched the edge of the milky blue blade and he had been cut instantly to the bone. Cavahn had to stitch the wound and apply antiseptic root for several days. He had never touched the blade again, always admiring it from a distance.

The supplicant turned in her chair to look at the NighT Guardian and Cavahn and in a moment appeared transfixed. Then she looked at her still tightly balled fists and brought them to her mouth and kissed the knuckles on each hand. She slowly rose; as she did she moved the chair back. Facing Cavahn's direction but without looking at her, the supplicant fell to her knees, her tightly balled fist stretched out in front of her as she extended herself to full length on the verandah floor, her forehead touching the floor as she tried to make her self as flat as possible. The supplicant was prostrate in front of Cavahn, her winged angel.

Around the corner of the table, Lovan looked on dumbfounded, still in his drying cloth. At the door to the verandah Vella appeared with a breakfast tray and simply stopped.

Silence.

No movement. Barely a breath passed the NighT Guardians lips, more than anything he was used to ritual and observance, dedication and expressions of obedience. At no time in his life had he thought of prostrating himself in front of anyone, especially not Cavahn.

There was acute awareness and tension in the air, somehow magnified by the resonating buzzing sound of the plants as liquid moved through them.

Although she was barefoot, their mother stood taller and more regal, blessed with an authority they had never seen. Like an audience, they froze to witnesses the events unfolding, and they were aware they were witnessing something few rarely see.

"Get up! Sit, I do not need your observance!" Cavahn said softly but firmly taking a moment to look at her spouse, and at Vella standing with a tray of food. She motioned her daughter to place the tray on the table and signaled to her son that he could go and change out of the drying cloth. He stared at her and signaled back that he would not; he did not want to miss anything. Which brought a smile to the corner of her mouth.

The supplicant had moved into a sitting position on the floor with her legs crossed and her balled fists resting on her knees. In all of her movements she had been completely silent and careful not to look in the direction of her Winged Angel.

"At the Table!" Cavahn uttered the words with an edge to her voice far sharper than the edge of the blade on her belt. The NighT Guardian visibly flinched at the way the three words were spoken, Lovan's eyes opened wide as he looked at his mother and Vella jostled the tray she was carrying causing some of bowls to clink together.

The supplicant scrambled to get from the floor to her chair, again avoiding all eye movement in the direction of her Winged Angel.

As Vella set the bowls of food in front of the supplicant she saw she was a girl, perhaps just past 20 years and was visibly shaking, her hands were balled so tightly into fists the nails on two of her fingers had dug into her palm and blood was about to drip off her hand. Vella reached for an unused meal cloth and tried to take the supplicants hand to clean the blood but found the balled fists and arms so taught and rigid they felt like carved wood. She looked over her shoulder at her mother.

"The supplicant will eat! The supplicant will be tended to!" Cavahn uttered the words in the same, sharp blade like tone. "You are mine now!" The supplicant followed Cavahn's words weakly with "I am yours." Cavahn moved to the table and looked at the shaking girl. "Whom did you belong to before? Who set such fear into you?"

The girl did not answer immediately, when she did, she said only "Garfan."

In that word hung a smell of violence and brutal obedience. Across the known lands, there was one universal way of observing and honoring all living things, life, nature, and spiritual goodness existing in all things and all people. It was a comforting belief system, light on rigid practice and adherence; anyone could meet, understand and practice the belief system in a way that pleased them.

For those who sought a stricter and more structured approach, worshipful orders had appeared, they were organized, held themselves separate from the world and became powerful in their own right. A few like the order of Garfan became synonymous with a brutally strict regime.

Cavahn stood behind the chair she had been sitting in and ran her hands along the intricate open carving of the chair she had been sitting in to eat breakfast. She moved to sit down which monetarily placed her within a short distance of the girl, which caused the girl to shake violently. As Cavahn sat down she said a number "1, I am 1".

The supplicant somehow became more rigid and frozen than she had been when Vella started tending her. In the realm of the worshipful orders, the orders simply known by a number were the oldest, and they wielded the most influence and power. The worshipful order of "1" was the oldest of all orders, and held the most of everything, power, wealth, influence and the most telling, ways of training for combat and obedience that left no marks on the follower. They were the only worshipful order that practiced the art of tattooing to declare their order and especially the ink that raised the skin and had been used to create Cavahn's wings.

Then, without warning the supplicant burst into tears and her entire body shook violently as she cried. Vella sat on the arm of the chair and hugged and comforted the supplicant who fell almost into her lap. Lovan ran his fingers through his long hair and slumped back into his chair and stared at the ceiling confused, relieved and shocked. Although wise in the way of politics, the military and feuding houses, he had simply overlooked the things he had heard about his mother.

The NighT Guardian still standing where he stopped moved to Cavahn's side, she held out a hand for him to take and smiled up at him "Yes my lover, I am 1" she said, with a warmth and tenderness they only used when alone together in the bedroom upstairs, or in a reed dome by the river. She brought his hand to her lips and kissed it.

The supplicant reached out her freshly bandaged hand and grasped a spoon, with her other still shaky hand, she grasped a small bowl and poured its contents into a larger one and started to mix the ingredients. She raised the bowl and its mixture to her chest and held it there. She started spooning small amounts of food into her mouth, slowly at first, then with greater speed and fuller spoons.

Vella sat down and stared at her mother. Lovan slowly turned his face down from looking at the ceiling and looked at his mother and then at the supplicant, as he did he pulled the drying cloth around him as if sheltering from something, he knew not what.

The NighT Guardian took his seat at the right hand of Cavahn, hands loosely folded in front of him and with a plain expression on his face; occasionally he would look at the supplicant as she ate.

Throughout the supplicants eating there was not a sound. The spoon in her hand did not seem to touch the bowl and no bowls clinked or made noise when they were set back on the table. Finally, she finished her meal and noiselessly moved her chair back from the table a distance far enough that she could not touch it.

The supplicant sat with her hands folded in her lap, staring straight ahead; if she were breathing there was no indication of it.

After several minutes Cavahn broke the silence that connected them all…. "You are mine, are you not?"

The supplicant nodded and said simply, "Yes."

"I admire your table manners, not a sound from eating." Said Cavahn.

"Thank you" responded the supplicant, "I have learned as well as I am able. And always." she hesitated, "To do what I can to honour my order, who owns me, and whom I serve."

The NighT Guardian studied the supplicant out of the corner of his eye, Lovan sat almost facing the girl and had a much better view and was studying her intently. Vella sat back and watched the dynamics around the table, especially her mother, she had always known in her heart that her mother was more than a mother and a lover for her father. Knowing from her mother's own lips that she was "1" changed everything.

As they watched each other around the table and listened to the questions flowing back and forth between Cavahn and the painfully worded responses of the supplicant; so meticulously worded were the answers and so even her voice, that both appeared to be connected by something far deeper in the girl's spirit.

With the suddenness of a knife blade the NighT Guardian changed the flow of questions "When were you last beaten?" Cavahn stared at the NighT Guardian, yes, she thought very perceptive of him, the Garfan order were renowned for brutal strictness, the complete opposite of her own. They administered punishment regularly, and often with no apparent reason she had heard.

The supplicant became immediately rigid in her chair. "It was 3 months ago, before I was sent to you!"

"Why? Who?" Questioned Cavahn, "How bad was the beating?"

Still rigid in her chair, staring straight ahead, in a level tone the supplicant answered. "I tended the flowering plants the monastery sold to raise money for food, two pots of plants died and could not be sold. I was beaten by three priests, I was beaten until I was unconscious."

The supplicant opened her mouth to speak further but Cavahn raised a finger from the arm of her chair and the supplicant immediately shut her mouth. It was not that this happened that surprised the NighT Guardian and Lovan; it was that they could not conceive of how the supplicant from her position could be aware Cavahn had raised her finger.

"My daughter at the end of the table is a superior doctor in the Imperial Service. She will examine you and report to me." Cavahn looked at the supplicants hat, cloak and boots, the sleeping roll and backpack she had with her. "How were you to travel?"

"I was instructed to walk only during Day Rise." Answered the supplicant. At this all of them looked at the girl with a mixture of surprise, disbelief, and admiration.

"So," continued Cavahn. "You were expected to die on your journey?"

For the first time the supplicant lowered her head and looked down at her bare feet. "Yes" she said quietly. Then she continued, "But my spirit is strong and my spirit guardians are strong also, I would not allow myself pass on, their faith in me and my faith in them are like a circle, the circle gave me strength." The supplicant paused and then continued, "I had been gifted to a winged angel who is a 1. There is no greater honour, it… " She stammered for a moment, "... such a rare, very rare honour."

Cavahn rested her head on one hand and looked at the supplicant. "You are acceptable." Cavahn paused. "You are in the house of a "1" now, this is my family and there are children not present who you will meet sometime." Cavahn paused again, "Are you able to bare children?" she asked.

The supplicant took the first breath anyone had seen. "Yes!" The word was a pronounced slowly, and clearly.

The three family members looked at Cavahn, wondering about the purpose of the question. But she was looking directly at Vella and making a hand signal at the side of her face the supplicant could defiantly not see.

Vella noisily, embarrassingly so, pushed back her chair and stood, she walked around to the supplicant and gently took the girls bandaged hand. The supplicant did not look at her; she stared straight ahead and rose from her chair, still without looking at Vella or anyone at the table and allowed herself to be led into the house.

Lovan spoke first and quietly to his mother, "I don't understand being beaten unconscious for allowing two plants to die!" Two questions from the NighT Guardian followed. "Traveling only during Day Rise, and what was that about bearing children?"

Cavahn adjusted her long dress. "The Holy order of 'Garfan' is renowned in the very far west and south for accepting the worst of children, or children from parents who can no longer afford to keep them. They use brutality to 'mold' the children into priests, monks and some girls, and boys will be used to provide surrogate fathers and mother's to families who cannot have their own children, but can pay." She stopped for a moment; "Boys and girls are selected before they are 25 years of age to be surrogates, after they are 25 they follow a worshipful path to the end of their lives unless some other need arises such as surrogate parent to replace a father or mother that has passed on."

The NighT Guardian said simply, "They sent her on a journey of almost three months, traveling only in the heat of the day and by her knowledge, they expected her to die on the road. What sort of order is that?"

Cavahn adjusted her seating cushion into a more comfortable position. "Yes, they did, and the duration of the journey means she must have started soon after that beating. As a girl who can bare children the order gave up a lot of potential income from surrogate motherhood."

Cavahn looked along the table and out in the garden baking in the Day Rise heat. "That is not what concerns me," she said. "Did you see?" She looked down at her finger and felt the other's eyes move to it, she raised it the same small degree she had when she had signaled to the supplicant. "Such a small motion of my finger and yet while staring at the wall ahead of her, and two chairs away, she was able to see, understand and react to it. In all orders, there are those who are chosen and trained to a degree of awareness that takes them to the very limit of existence in this physical world. I think we will find she has been greatly abused in her order but she has also been trained to the limit of what her physical being is aware of."

The NighT Guardian looked at his son and then at his spouse, "Then if she is as you say, she could have easily traveled such a great distance in the heat of Day Rise."

"Absolutely! Cavahn replied. "The journey and the way it had to be carried out was the final test assigned to her, and it was a test that if she failed she would be dead and we would never know it was attempted."

"I'm sorry, I don't understand," said Lovan. "Until she arrived, no one…." He paused and looked at his mother. "You knew she was coming, before she arrived," he blurted out. His eyes widened a little.

His mother looked at him for several seconds, "I knew three days ago, as she was crossing The Black Bridge over the lower river, her pace was fast, brutally unrelenting. Her entire being was dedicated to maintaining the pace required for her to be here today. So dedicated was her essence, her spirit in this world vibrated, that was how I first knew she was coming."

For a moment the NighT Guardian's jaw sagged and then he shut it quickly. He had heard of such people as was now being described, he had always thought of them as being stories, told to children to keep them in their place. A mother would tell her child she could hear or see what they were doing at the Educator or when playing a little too far from home, or on a clambering frame they were not allowed to use because it was too high, or when running through the market trying to pick up fruit at the edge of a vendors table when the containing mesh was down. As he had grown older, it was said very wealthy families would pay for the privilege of having such a person at their castle or in the army as it campaigned so as to get an advantage over an enemy, but he had never seen it. "She referred to you as a winged angel, I thought it referred to your tattoos." He said.

A wry smile crossed Cavahn's lips, "My lover, that is true, and the wings are a permanent mark of the highest level attainable."

Trying to grasp the magnitude of the gifts Cavahn had he wondered how things would change now. "How should we treat you now that we know all this… about you, your order? I feel as if I should venerate you in some way." He said unsure now of how to speak to Cavahn.

"Nothing changes my lover" she looked him directly in the eyes "I will continue to gather roots, clean and slice them for you to eat when you stand guard. I will continue to build domes down in the reeds by the water and spend hours naked with you copulating. I will clean and prepare your robes for guard duty." Then she turned to look her son in the eyes "I am still your mother."

A smile crossed The NighT Guardian's lips. Cavahn saw it, "So, now, what brings that smile?"

He frowned that his smile had been noticed; though now he felt there is no way it could not have been missed. "I" he stopped for a moment and then continued so as to honour his honesty. "I like the fact you will still build domes down by the river and we will spend time in them!"

Cavahn laughed easily… "You always did think with your cock! Yes, there will be many, many more domes built. And, we will have long special moments when our spirits fly free and join together!"

Vella emerged from inside the house and moved to stand beside her mother's chair, she ran her hand across some of her mother's tattoos, those that could be touched through the intricate carving in the back of her chair. She looked at her father, "An interesting conversation, I can't imagine you would not know how special the angel sitting here is. Since I was a little girl I have watched you in the shower with us caring for, and wondering at the tattoos." She smiled at her father and her brother. "Just as we talked last night, some of the most amazing things are hidden in plain sight!" Then she moved to sit at the table, next to her father who turned to her as she sat, "You knew about your mother. How long have you known?" He demanded.

Before Vella could reply the NighT Guardian looked across at his son "I have always thought they were the most incredible tattoos and wondered at how and why they were done. But I never put those thoughts into words." He paused, "I have marveled at the gift of laying next to your mother in the night and listening to her breathe and watching our children – you, come from her. The time we spend down by the river, the conversations late into the night. So many things but never have I questioned any deeper." The NighT Guardian looked back at Vella and then at Cavahn. For the first time in his life, he felt lost, a world of meaning had existed in front of his eyes and he had not seen it. And now, he had so much to learn.

Cavahn reached out and rubbed his cheek with the back of her hand. "It is not that something was hidden, no question was asked and no answer volunteered. My order is not one to hide things; we prefer they be in plain site and answer questions as they are asked." She stood and walked to his side and put her arm around his shoulder and bent to kiss his forehead, as she did, his powerful arms circled tightly encircled her waist.

The NighT Guardian started to sob as he released his feelings, for 30 years, he had not questioned or thought or said a word about what he saw every day but which could have added more meaning and nuances to their lives in those years.

The supplicant emerged from inside of the house, she was barefoot, and she no longer wore the clothes she arrived in. Now she wore clothes donated by Vella. A pair of dark blue pants which were slightly too long for her, they were turned up maybe two or three times at the ankles, a clean white blouse. The sleeves also turned up several times at the cuffs, on her belt, her knife.

The supplicant looked to her left, to the breakfast table where sat Cavahn, her winged angel. All others had gone somewhere inside, there would just be herself and Cavahn who had changed also. She now wore a long dark maroon dress with blue and gold piping, the back was not open, and her wings were not on show. She too was bare foot; at her waist she wore her knife. Her blade sat on her waist in such a way that it was easily reached by her left, blade, hand.

The supplicant saw this and the metal bracelet on the winged angel's left wrist and forearm; it covered all of the wrist and most of the forearm. It looked like elaborate jewelry but in reality it was a wrist shield that protected the wearer's lower arm in the event of a blade fight.

The Supplicant paused in her movements and looked at the searing heat of Full Day Rise and how it caused the air to shimmy and vibrate. Slowly, she took from her belt her blade and set it on the floor to one side of the doorway. No matter how good her training in blade combat she could not start to imagine any outcome of a fight with a winged angel that would not result in her death. That must not be allowed to happen.

She continued to walk to the edge of the verandah floor to the edge where the heat of day rise beat down and opened her hands, with the palms facing upwards and fingers spread wide she reached forward and exposed them to the heat bearing down from the two suns. She stood there with her one hand naked and exposed to the suns and one bandaged hand partly exposed for a short time period, breathing deeply all the while.

She brought her hands back from exposure to Day Rise and held the palms up to study them, the ritual of Cleansing by Day Rise had been completed. The winged angel motioned for her to approach. The supplicant stopped at arms length from Cavahn and held out her hands for inspection.

The supplicant's hands had been cleansed by Full Day Rise but told the Winged Angel an immense amount of information about the girl. The fingers were long and slender like her own and no doubt were capable of the same fierce, formidable grip. The insides of the thumb and palm of her right hand had calluses and hard skin from years of training with her blade, she was right handed with her knife. For a moment Cavahn's mind went back to her days training against right-handed enemies. The sort of training this girl endured had changed the very shape of the handle of her blade. Cavahn could see that it would now be molded so tightly to her hand that anyone else would have trouble holding it and being effective with it, the blade would be an extension of the hand and arm of the person wielding it. The training at Cavahn's order differed, her blade was equally unique to her own hand from sustained, hard training but her hand would never show the hard skin and calluses that would give away her knowledge and ability with the weapon at her waist.

The supplicant's left hand was quite different. It showed thin, broken, wavering purple lines along the index finger and little finger. Cavahn knew that the supplicants order practiced the use of natural drugs that would enhance the users ability, stamina, mental agility, vision, and hearing, control of the heart or breath. The drugs were administered by a few grains of powder on the side of the index and the little finger and they left a tell tale stain for a few hours. The Winged Angel indicated the supplicant should sit in the chair immediately in front of her.

The supplicant looked at the chair as if it were an executioner's trap that had been set for her. When seated as directed her knees would almost be touching Cavahn's knees. The way the Cavahn was sitting, all she had to do was flex her knees, this would bring her feet off the floor directly on to the supplicants shins, pushing them back violently and up under the chair, causing the girls knees to explode with pain – the distraction. The motion of her legs and the distracting pain would cause her to pitch forward. The motion would bring her very close to Cavahn, who only had to draw her knife and plunge it into the supplicant's throat and brain, killing her instantly.

The supplicant sat down.

The questions, Cavahn said, would be quickly delivered and the answers the supplicant would be expected to give would be equally quickly answered. A delay in answering could bring death as easily as the wrong answer. An answer judged to be correct only guaranteed life until the next question.

"Your Name?" Cavahn asked the question with such a feint, quiet, voice, the supplicant was taken off guard. She had expected a something different, her order had never prepared her for this situation, they had never trained her but they had talked of it. They referred to it as "the facing" a time and a place chosen by who she was given to that would strip away all, nothing could hide even in the deepest corner of her soul. "Pendal" she replied. And then she screamed.

At the utterance of her name Cavahn reached out with the hand opposite to her blade hand and seized the supplicants hand, and pulled, twisting and leveraging all at the same time. The grip and motion were excruciatingly painful. The pain spread rapidly through her entire arm up to her shoulder. She had not anticipated this; she had expected her legs to be the painful distracting target.

"Why, Pendal?" Whispered Cavahn. Pendal breathed deeply to manage the pain that was locking her arm and spreading into her shoulder, neck, and down to her chest. As the pain moved so the body where it passed became immobile. Even her breathing to manage her pain caused more pain; she was becoming frozen like a statue. She started to struggle to breathe.

She looked down at the source of the pain, Cavahn's grip on her, and saw no hand, Cavahn was sitting back in her chair, watching. Pendal was contorted, fixed in her chair, and the position Cavahn had placed her. Slowly dying. Pendal started to cry; this had also been spoken of. Someone could cause pain in a way that persons own body perpetuated it until a blessed release was offered. Pendal' s tears started to flood down her face.

"I do not know why I was gifted!" Pendal struggled to form the words using precious breathes for each one.

"You will die," said Cavahn sitting comfortably in her chair, her eyes locked in Pendal's dimming eyes.

"No!" the word was torn from the small amount of air still in Pendal's lungs. She was only vaguely aware of Cavahn reaching out and tapping on her breastbone. As her eyes closed she thought of her death but air surged into her lungs; her chest moved and heaved to gather more air. When she opened her eyes, she could breathe but the pain was spreading across her ribs and back, her legs hung useless from the chair.

"Why?" the question floated on the still cool air between where they sat and reverberated of the burning hot air just at the edge of the verandah.

"I do not know why!" Pendal repeated the words. As she did Cavahn reached forward and placed the backhand of her non-blade hand on the opposite side of Pendal's forehead, momentarily covering her third eye. An explosion of colour!

Colours everywhere, all shades and hues, colours she had not seen before and could not think even existed, as she watched the colours the pain receded into the back of her mind and the colours started to form shapes, shapes became people and a house, a pet animal she had when she was young.

Being young was confusing. The young person she saw in her mind looked like her and talked with her dialect but the hair was lighter and shorter, this young person was playing in a clean open space, with animals, a small tame Vanmor and other small animals. The Pendal in her mind was happy! That is what was confusing, she had been happy, once.

"I was happy," she said the words softly and slowly as the images continued to play across her mind.

"Not in this life" replied Cavahn. "What you see in your mind is a past life. Your life sprit existed then and was happy. I doubt we will find the answer of your gifting to me in your current life, something from a past life that is so driving you in this one that we must look there."

Pendal gasped… years were passing now in front of her eyes. She had grown and the Vanmor was old and slow now, the thick fur at its neck was white and its head hung a little lower. It had lost one of its fangs. The small animals she had been playing with as a little girl were gone, they had died and been replaced with others with different colour fur. The light was clear and clean; it was that time between Night Set and Day Rise when all was still except for… for the VodaKex raiders.

VodaKex raiders, a disenfranchised sect of House VodaKhan would occasionally raid northern crop growers, taking food, trinkets and sometimes people. They were angry with VodaKhan for throwing them out of the parent sect, they were angry with the crop growers because they were settled had families and some wealth and were happy. They were angry because they had no crops and no gold and no status. It was said they were also angry at the suns and moons above their heads.

Blood on the ground her father's blood. He was dead. He appeared to be standing, leaning against the side of Pendal's home, a weapon lay at his feet, his head rested on his chest, a throwing spear was buried deep in his chest and into the side of the house by the front door. It was the spear through his body and wedged into the house that held him up and made it appear as if he was standing. Behind Pendal stood her mother, her mother's hands on the girl's shoulders.

Raiders emerged from the house with an odd collection of the family's possessions. The largest and most beautiful was an icon depicting the spirit of that tended to the needs of plants, like the ones they harvested and which sustained them and their community in the dark nights of winter. It had been a gift from the priest at the nearby religious order for donations of crops to the poor who had no food. There was a drawer of her mothers eating utensils; she had brought them to the house when she had married her farmer husband.

There were some of Pendal's toys, precious toys she had played with as she grew up. It was said VodaKex children only had toys taken from others. The children would play with the toys but were also taught to despise those whom the toys had been taken from as being weak and unable to protect what they had. Pendal screamed a curse at the raider holding her toys.

The raider stopped in mid stride as if surprised and stung by the curse words, slowly, gently he laid the toys on the table where the family would sit outside at night in the cool air and talk about the day, and eat their evening meal. At meals end they would talk about the tasks for the day to come and simply enjoy each other's company. Boys, in rags probably stolen on other raids were taking anything laid on the table and storing it in bags for riding animals to carry back north.

The raider by the table looked at Pendal and her mother, pointed at them and grunted to a tall leader at the gate to the house. The leader studied them and nodded. In that moment the raiders had decided Pendal and her mother were to be taken and owned by the thief of Pendal's toys.

Pendal screamed more curse words as the raider seized her and her mother by an arm. Pendal had a short blade in the sash of her belt; she used it for working with the plants and killing river creatures she caught when she went down to he river to collect water or bathe. As the raider tugged at her arm he pulled Pendal off balance causing her free arm to come across her body and her knife hand to fall on the handle of her blade. Without thought and with no training on how to kill a person she seized the blade handle and her slim, young girls arm, allowed her to bring the blade up inside the raiders chest defender and into his chest.

The blade found the raiders heart and cut it in two.

The Raider yelled in surprise, pain and pulled back from Pendal. As he lurched away from Pendal the motion and weight of his body pulled the blade out of Pendal's hand, jamming between his body and the inside of his chest defender.

She was defenseless, weak, in front of the raiders.

With the last air in his lungs the raider shouted the alert and fell backwards on to the table smashing the tray of toys Pendal had wanted to protect. She could not guard her mother or herself now.

To her right and behind, Pendal heard a sound like a big bag of field roots hit the ground. She turned to look for the source of the sound and saw her mother face down on the ground a gushing red stain in the middle of her back and the tip of a raider blade red with blood. Pendal felt a heavy impact in the middle of her own back that pushed her violently to one side. She thought of her brother in that moment, he was gone to the south, to be in the army of a great house. He would surprise her with a big slap in her back, which would make her scream, and then she would chase after him to hit him and pull his hair when eventually Pendal caught him. There was pain now in her chest; she looked down to see a throwing spear erupted from her chest, its point covered in her blood glistening in the early morning light. Her legs were weakening, her knees landed in liquid on the ground, it splashed up on her dress, it was red, with all her ebbing strength she looked for her mother's face, the liquid on the ground was not river liquid, it was her mother's blood, Pendal could no fathom how much was pouring form her mother's brutal wound.

Pendal tried to scream but her there was no energy, and no air in her lungs now. She twitched like a rag doll toy as the throwing spear was jerked out of body. Her knees rested now on the hard pre winter, frozen, ground and abruptly there was no pain just the sound of air from gurgling with her blood from the hole the spear had made in her chest.

Pendal placed a hand on her mother's shoulder as her strength left her, for a moment she rested, with her other hand she slipped under the back of her mother's dress, one more time she thought, one more time to run her hand over the raised wing tattoos on her mothers back. All Pendal could feel in the last moments were regret, terrible regret at her unintended action, terrible regret at her lack of skill and focus on the moment… her toys were nothing compared to the life of her mother, her mother was so, so vital, a winged angel, so rare, so full of life and she had killed her angel that birthed and loved her.

Pendal fell across her mother, dead.

"My mother was a Winged Angel!" gasped Pendal.

"Yes"

"What have you learned?" questioned Cavahn.

"I am gifted to you, to learn from you." There was clarity in her words and her vision of her life's purpose. It was clear to her now that the pain and suffering she had endured in her order, the beatings, punishment and brutal training regime had been there to create from an innocent girl, a human weapon that would not be defenseless simply because she lost her blade in a fight. The event of that early morning in a past life would never be repeated in this one, or other lives to come.

Cavahn studied Pendal for a moment, noting how the pain raged through her body, the question had been answered but a gift like Pendal was given not for what was past, that was finished, complete, and could not be changed. No, Pendal was gifted for things her spirit was to learn and would be useful in the present, and the future. Cavahn leaned forward and kissed Pendal on the lips. In that moment she took away Pendal's pain.

Pendal's body fell from the chair, she was unconscious before she hit the floor. Cavahn stepped over the fallen girl and walked into the house.

The NighT Guardian studied Pendal from the entrance to his home. It was late Day Rise; temperatures were not so intense outside the coolness of the verandah. Pendal stood naked at the edge of the verandah; the clothes gifted her by Vella lay very neatly folded on the verandah floor. Pendal was holding her hands out in to the failing heat, first palms up and then palms down, each time she changed hands she said a prayer to her guardian spirits. There were four verses to the prayer, each day she would have four things she would be thankful for, two each for her guardians. It was an act of cleansing and organizing her thoughts and enjoyment about the day. She was connecting with her guardian spirits.

The NighT Guardian noted the scars on the girl's legs, arms and back. Some were cuts, some were puncture wounds and there was one, long, livid purple scar that curled up her back and across and over her right shoulder, the shoulder of her blade hand.

The scars were clearly collected over time, some from training sessions, he knew they were training scars because the scars were in places that would have been fatal if the weapon that made them had pressed all the way home. Her trainer had been extremely skilled and had held back, only cutting deep enough to give pain, draw blood and leave a scar but not deep enough to maim or kill. It was intended she would bear the marks on her body for her life as ways to remember having failed in some way and to learn from them and the painful period of healing after the cut or puncture.

And, he noted she had learned, no scar was repeated. It made him ashamed of the multiple scars in the same place on his blade arm; he had been a slow learner when he was her age.

She was lean and hard muscled. In a fight she would be lithe, fast and quick. He agreed with Cavahn's report that she was a weapon; if Pendal were disarmed he was sure she could still press an attack and be lethal in its execution.

He reflected on the great distance she had covered to be with them and the pace she had maintained to achieve her goal. It was not so much the vast distance and amount of time it took her, or rather the short amount of time. The journey was the last training session her mentor had assigned her, during the journey she had honed her endurance, fitness and above all her concentration and single-mindedness. To travel such distance in a short time required a mind that focused on an outcome and drove the body to make it happen. The body was made to be obedient to the mind; a twisted ankle, though unlikely in the boots she was wearing, would not delay her; the pain of the injury would be pushed to the back or even out of her mind as her mind drove the body onward. The journey required a relentless sustained pace day after day after day to meet the mind's goal and that had been sustained.

He turned and walked inside leaving Pendal to her cleansing.

He met Cavahn at the foot of the stairs; she stopped on the bottom step and looked at him. "She is Day Cleanings and praying to her guardian spirits" he said. She nodded, "Naked." It was a statement, not a question. "Yes, he responded."

Cavahn paused, "What do you think?"

"Hard bodied, very fit and strong, lithe, and brutally fast in a fight. None of her training scars have been repeated, she has learned from being cut by her trainer." He paused, "I am sure she knows multiple unbladed forms of combat and ways to kill. Being without a blade merely changes the way she fights and kills." He took a deep breath, "I would find it a challenge to win a fight with her." He looked at Cavahn's bare feet. "She is like you, only you, of all of us, could fight her with assurance of victory."

Cavahn ran her fingers through his hair, "You underestimate yourself, don't forget, you have been in the Vanguard, you have fought many battles and won them all."

He held Cavahn's hand and kissed the inside of her wrist. "That maybe, but she is very much like you. I have watched you train every day for years remember? I helped you give birth to Invar on the floor of the training room. We cleaned up the birth fluids and I held our daughter while you completed your training session. You are more focused and able than she is."

"I suppose I am, I had forgotten about where and what was happening when Invar was birthed" she took a deep breath. "Pendal is here for a purpose, she is made and equipped with skills that are meant to be useful for that purpose." She looked at the NighT Guardian. "I must train with her and understand her, a lot is revealed in a fierce training session, the true meaning of a person appears then."

Darkness.

Almost darkness.

The Training room; the thick reed mat that usually covered the floor it had been turned back revealing hard stone that glistened now from careful oiling. The lighting globes had been turned off, instead, suspended on ropes from the ceiling in highly decorative black metal holders candles burned. Above the candleholders a mechanism ticked imperceptibly. After an allotted period of time it would lower a cover over the candleholders that would force their light into a small, tight, circular pools on the floor.

The NighT Guardian stared at the floor, yes it was true that he had fought many battles and had won them all, he was alive to prove it and his body though scarred and slightly out of shape where the bones had been broken, was whole but he had never trained in this room or in the way he was to give witness.

This was to be a unique session; partly a test for Pendal, partly a training session but mostly he reflected confirmation of Cavahn's abilities.

The worshipful orders Cavahn and Pendal came from practiced a belief that true perfection in the fighting arts required supreme balance, agility, power and relentless pursuit of the opponent. The floor was a perfect example. Polished and oiled just a short while before, he would never dare walk on it let alone train or fight on it. Yet that is what Cavahn and Pendal were about to do. This would also be a test of their ability to sense an opponent and reach out and make contact with another's spiritual essence in the steadily darkening room.

At one corner he could just make out Cavahn, at the other Pendal, they stood on small wooden platforms, about knee height above the floor. On the platform there was just enough space for them to have their feet side by side. They were identically dressed. Tight form fitting, dull black suits from head to toe, even their hands were covered, the feet were covered but open at the bottom for the bare skin to make contact with the slick floor. Their heads and faces were covered, the face with a mesh allowing breathing and vision. In their knife hand each held a hard stiff "knife" made from hard reeds, tree wood, and leather.

No blood would be spilled from the knives, there would be no cuts and no blood spilled from the knives but the welts and bruises left on an opponents body from contact with an opponent's "knife" would be one way they would score the score the fight. Hands and feet – kicking and punching, were allowed, and drawing blood from a punch or kick to the face definitely occurred. If an opponent surrendered, by giving their blade to their opponent, that was another way of scoring the fight, but if the opponent had skills that allowed them to continue without a blade, using complex and agile kicks, fists and other brutal bodily contacts, they would continue until one could fight no longer.

Like the NighT Guardian, Vella sat wedged into a corner of the room. Each sat on a one legged stool, bracing of their legs and pushing their bodies into the corner kept them from falling over.

A peg, the size of a finger dropped from its holder to the floor. The peg was made from a hard reed, it was chosen because it did not bounce when it hit the floor; its angular shape stopped it from rolling. The sharp sound of it meeting the floor signaled the start of the contest.

No movement, Cavahn and Pendal staid rooted to their pedestals.

Waiting.

Silence.

No movement.

Pendal was making the first move.

She leapt from her pedestal landing fully one third of the way across the stone-fighting floor. Her bare feet contacted with the slick oiled stone surface but did not slip or make a sound. She crouched low, perfectly balanced, her knife in her non-knife hand and highly visible and aligned along the forearm of.

The NighT Guardian was surprised at the simplicity of the move; the leap was intended to carry her sliding across the floor quickly and with minimal effort, and the position of the knife was predictable. An opponent might see – no, was intended to see the knife blade and fix their attention on it. They would miss the fact the handle was just showing from Pendal's hand. An attack or defensive move made to that side, where they saw the blade would fail. In the last moment Pendal would seize the handle in her knife hand and change the entire balance of her body and its muscular power.

A classic, simple move; expose the weapon, lure an attack to where the weapon is perceived to be and at the last moment switch the weapon to the other side and attack with it while the opponent is trying to adjust to the change in where the threat comes from.

Pendal was so fast the NighT Guardian thought he had seen a spirit move.

He had stood guard one night after a battle, and through the night mist and smoke from burning war machines he thought he saw dark figures moving across the battlefield. He had stared and stared into the darkness trying to see if the shapes were spirit guardians of fallen soldiers collecting their souls for transport to the next life. In his mind, the desperate cries of the wounded who knew they would die that night on the cold, blood soaked battlefield became the cries of souls and spirits, unwilling, or too terrified, to move to the next life being pulled from dying physical bodies by spirit guardians.

According to a soldiers belief, if a spirit was not collected or did not go willingly to the next life on the night they fell in battle, their spirit would be trapped in the corpse until year end, when, on two a special nights when no moons appeared in the night sky, they could finally move to the next life.

As the mists and clouds hiding second moon shifted and parted he could see nothing, just mangled bodies, and burnt out war machines.

Pendal was moving again, fast and low, at the edge of the training arena and lunging at the pedestal Cavahn stood on. The NighT Guardian had trust and confidence in Cavahn's ability to defeat Pendal but she was still standing motionless as if she had not heard the peg drop.

Pendal was still lunging forward and making a scything sweep at Cavahn's closest leg but as her knife moved brutally fast through the air, she made no contact. Cavahn had rotated on her opposite leg sweeping Pendal's target away. At the same time Cavahn appeared to let all strength drain from her standing leg, dropping her in to a squat so fast a stone could not move faster when dropped. The downward momentum of her body weight and the pirouette motion allowed her to place her entire weight and all its muscle power behind her knife as she brought it down on Pendal's right shoulder, the shoulder of the arm in which Pendal held her knife.

Silence.

The sound of the knife making contact with Pendal's unprotected shoulder was heard throughout the room, the fierceness of the impact startled the NighT Guardian into a state of wakefulness he had not experienced for a long time. Across the room, second daughter was transfixed by the speed, agility and power of her mother's blow.

Silence.

Pendal did not utter so much as a sharp intake of breath. She was already turning to her left to follow Cavahn who had stepped silently from her pedestal and taken up a central position on stone floor. As Pendal turned to follow Cavahn's movement she used the rotation of her body to help swing what now appeared to be a lifeless arm across her so that her left hand could take the knife from Pendal's right hand.

Cavahn stood silent and motionless waiting for Pendal's next move. The NighT Guardian reflected on what he had seen. If the knives had been for real, Pendal would be dead already; she would be bleeding out on the floor. A blade such as the milky blue one that Cavahn wore with honour and displayed in their bedroom would have cut Pendal's arm clean off together with part of her shoulder.

He marveled at the restraint and agility of his spouse. Pendal had been encouraged to attack by the apparent inaction of her opponent. There was a controlled urgency about

Pendal that the NighT Guardian now saw as her weakness. She had been trained to attack first, to seize the initiative and use it to put the opponent at a disadvantage, but she had never competed against an opponent such as Cavahn that did not see losing the initiative as a weakness. When Cavahn had said she wanted to find Pendal's limitations she meant both the girls physical prowess and her mind. The mind controls the body and the soul manifests the mind, so it is in all things, but even more so when physical life depends on it.

Pendal's was crouching and slightly bent over, she swung her injured right arm left and right as she moved forward, now she was swinging it in circles, using her body to give her arm motion. She was regaining feeling in the arm and shoulder and testing it for how useful it would be in the next engagement. And, damaged as it was, the twisting action and leverage of her torso would allow her to use the dead weight of her arm as like a crude club.

Silence.

Cavahn studied Pendal's actions and motion. As Pendal moved to her right Cavahn moved left and shortened the distance between them.

Blackness.

The mechanism holding the shades above the two candles had reached its preplanned time and dropped the shades over the candles. As the NighT Guardian's eyes struggled to adjust he saw the pale glow of the two tightly focused pools of light on the floor of the arena. Each pool of light, no bigger than one of Cavahn's thighs, was all that illuminated the room now.

The oil on the stone reflected the light only slightly now, inside the pools of light.

He watched as legs and a body crouched low moved across one a pool of light on the far side of the training room floor. Then again the same shape on his side of the floor. After each transit across a pool of light, there was the savage sound of a body, a person, being hit, beaten. And again, and again the figure transiting across the pools of light was the same, the slightly shorter legs of Pendal and a right arm and shoulder dropped low.

Like an erratically played drum the sound of a knife or a fist or a foot kissing an opponent with pain and injury beat off the walls and floor of the training room, the sounds always followed by movement across a pool of light. As he watched the nimbleness of Pendal's shadow movements grew less lithe and stealthy. There was never a hint of miss balance in her movements but the retreat was becoming less and less speedy and on one occasion, it was decidedly slow.

He never saw the longer muscled legs of his beloved Cavahn.

Silence continued to reign over the proceedings.

Then, there was a word, "Glimmer!" Spoken softly by Cavahn's voice. It signified the end. Pendal had not crossed either pool of light in her recognizable crouch for several minutes. She had not attacked.

The lighting globes slowly illuminated the training room in a warm orange, pre Day Rise glow.

Cavahn stood naked on her pedestal, her body covering neatly folded on the wooden floor beside the training floor. She gestured to the NighT Guardian; it was time for him to inspect her from head to foot for any evidence of a bruise or injury that would be counted in favour of Pendal, the opponent.

The NighT Guardian stood with difficulty, his legs had locked into the position of bracing his body in the corner on the one legged stool. The stool, now without his weight and bracing fell to the floor making a horrible loud and hard sound in the room, confused and embarrassed by what had happened the NighT Guardian looked for apology from Cavahn. He received none she stared straight ahead.

Leaving the stool rocking back and forth on the floor the NighT Guardian moved quickly to inspect Cavahn for injury. There was none.

As he looked at her back he saw the raised tattoos of her wings were far more prominent than he had ever seen before. The intricate tattoos now appeared to be a full finger width higher than the flat of her back. He ran his fingers across those he could reach and sensed a definite pulsing and bone like hardness and feather like softness. As he ran his fingers over more and more of the tattoos the pulsing grew less and less, and the raised tattoo grew less pronounced, returning to what he was used to seeing and touching in bed.

Cavahn stepped down from her pedestal and left the training room, the NighT Guardian turned to the scoring register behind Cavahn and set the white marker into it holder, an examination of Cavahn showed no evidence Pendal had scored any hit or even touched her opponent so the scoring marker was not required.

Vella walked awkwardly across the slick floor to kneel beside Pendal who lay sprawled on the training room floor struggling to get up, her legs and damaged shoulder continuously defeated her attempts on the slick surface. The NighT Guardian cautiously stepped out on the oiled floor and joined his daughter who was removing Pendal's body covering.

Blood ran from Pendal's nose and mouth. She moaned and grunted in agony as the body covering was removed. The shoulder struck by Cavahn in Pendal's first assault as already an intense, deep black and purple bruise. There were multiple bruises all over Pendal's body and she shivered uncontrollably. One eye was bruised closed. The left hand that had held her knife after her right was so badly bruised was damaged; possibly two or three fingers were broken. Pendal's leather and wood knife lay broken several feet from where she now bled.

With the NighT Guardian carrying Pendal's upper body and Vella carrying her legs they moved Pendal out of the training arena to the showers where they could wash her and Vella could inspect and treat the girl's injuries.

The NighT Guardian emerged into the failing light of late Day Rise. Cavahn sat in a large drying cloth at the table. Her feet on a footstool she wiggled her toes and examined her toe and fingernails. As he approached she held out a hand, he took it as he always did and kissed it.

"Thank you for witnessing" she said softly and kissed his hand.

He sat facing her. "I have never seen your abilities like this…" He stopped and reflected on what he had been able to see in the dim light of the training room, but mostly, what he had heard. He had heard the repeated contact of Cavahn on Pendal as she rebutted the girl's attacks and punishing her severally as she did. But then he reflected; the punishment she had received at Cavahn's hand was probably less than her mentor had meted out. He and Cavahn had trained together many times over the years especially when they first returned home from the west and after K'ola, their first daughter was birthed, but they had never trained on the slick floor he saw today, the floor had always been covered by a tough, padded, reed mat "…I only ever saw Pendal's silhouette moving across the floor. "

Cavahn lounged back in her chair and looked down at the floor very thoughtfully. It was a long time before she replied, the buzzing of the water moving in the plants had stopped because the heat of day Rise was ebbing and had been replaced by the chirping sounds of the small flying birds as they caught their fill of insects down in the reeds. The sound of the birds seemed to magnify the silence of Cavahn's thoughts.

Finally, without looking at the NighT Guardian, Cavahn replied. "Pendal's errors were not her's alone." Cavahn looked up directly at the NighT Guardian.

"Our spirit exists in physical bodies for many different lives… in those diverse lives the spirit learns many things and adds them to those of previous lives" Cavahn paused, waiting for the NighT Guardian to say something or make a gesture but he remained silent, unmoving, he simply wanted to hear what was next. "Our sprit, our essential essence, learns and enriches itself and in some cases, it endures hardship and immense sorrow. When the physical body is no more, our spirit passes into another body at birth and the process continues." Cavahn stopped to take a sip of river liquid. "When I questioned her out here…" Cavahn's right arm made a sweeping gesture indicating the whole verandah "I knew the answer to her existence today lay in a past life, one that probably had a tragic end… it was… a tragic end."

"Like our children she was once the daughter of a Winged Angel, her father was a farmer. She was born in the very far west and north. Her parents were well respected in their community but on one chilly pre winter day VodaKex raiders on their way back north for the winter raided her farm. Her father already dead she alone was left to protect herself and her mother."

Cavahn paused and took a deep breath. "A confrontation." She said softly, "One she could not win, it could only end in immense sorrow and her death."

"Whoever she was called in that life killed one of the raiders. In a moment of revenge the raiders killed her mother and then her. As she was dying she reached out to touch her mother's tattoos, and in those last moments she felt guilt and immense sadness that she could not protect her mother, her lack of training, for her lack of focus on what was around her, lack of focus on the fact her toys... yes, her childhood toys started it. On how she lacked control of her decisions, decisions that could lead to death and sorrow." Cavahn stopped and started drinking her river liquid.

"Penance" said the NighT Guardian.

Cavahn nodded.

"Penance, yes, the brutal regime of her order was a form of penance, her spirit was learning and enduring, and she was learning focus. She was learning control over her decisions, she was learning how to defend against almost any threat she could imagine. Allowing two plants to die was a lack of focus and it brought with it painful consequences, a beating. But, better than being dead and better than causing someone else to die."

Cavahn nodded and now held her glass of river liquid in both hands and rolled it back and forth swishing the remaining liquid around the inside of the glass.

"How would she have known you were here?" asked the NighT Guardian.

Silence.

Finally Cavahn replied. "I was the only one of my order to wed someone from the Vanguard, there were two others, but they joined with soldiers of the Legion. It would have been simple for a senior of the Garfan order to find out, perhaps through them." Cavahn looked up smiling, "A daughter of my order bonding with an officer from the Vanguard of the Imperial Black Legion is not a small thing." Cavahn set the glass down on the table upside down, a classic statement of completeness and emptiness at the same time.

Cavahn leaned forward, pushing the empty glass away from her. "The spirit in her young body is here to learn and evolve, today marked the end of her penance. Her soul needs to move on and to learn about what it means to be alive, in this life. That is why she is here, not for any thought she was protecting me. Today she found out I do not need it. Knowing what we know and being able to help her is part of our journey... She will join our family!" Cavahn looked at the NighT Guardian. "We have laughed about the idea of parenting another generation before we grow too old to do so. Maybe a generation of one, one that we do not have to conceive." She continued to look at the NighT Guardian for any sense of opposition or resistance to the idea.

There was none.